BASED ON A UBISOFT CREATION

IMMORTALS
FENYX RISING™

FROM GREAT BEGINNINGS

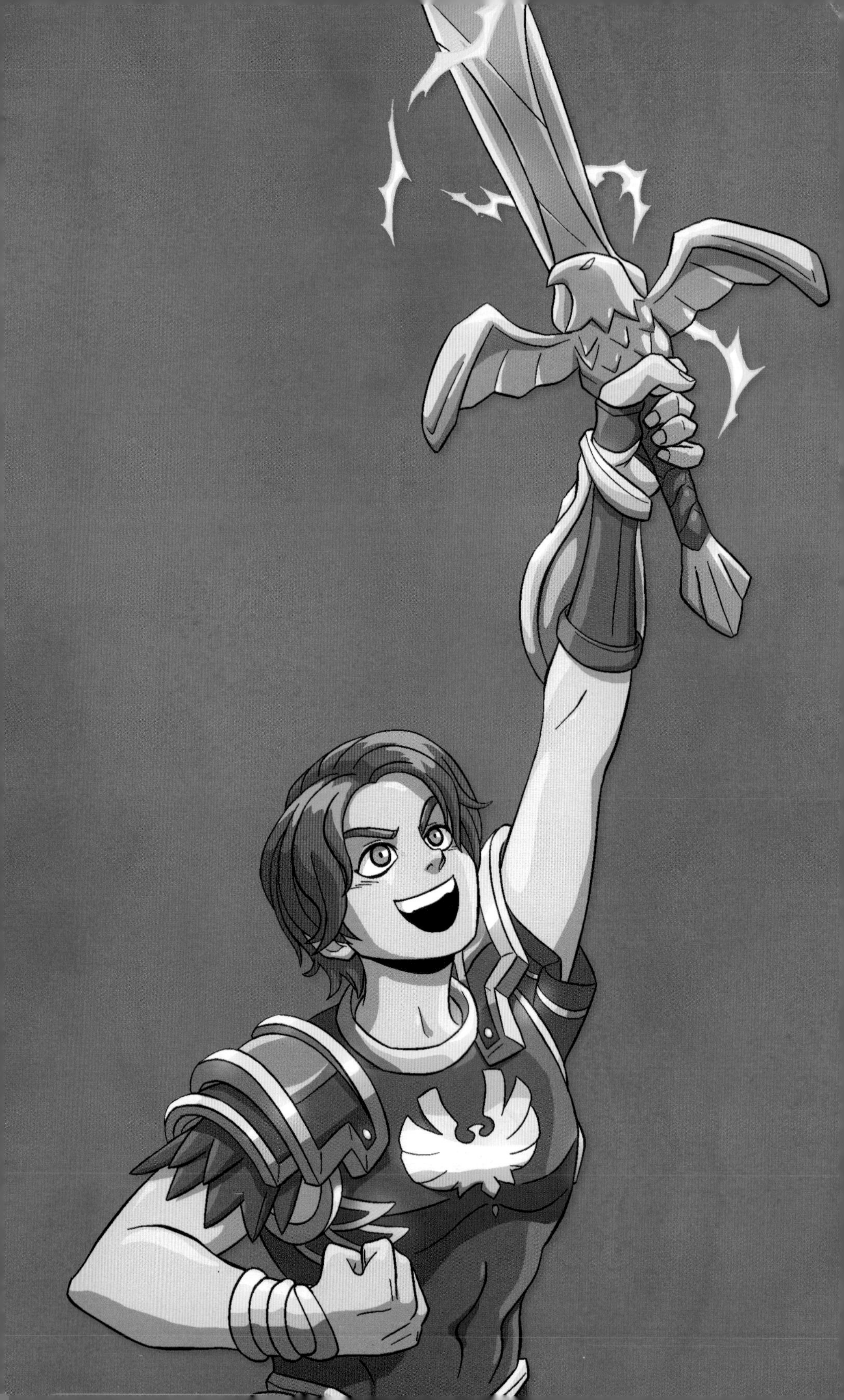

BASED ON A UBISOFT CREATION

IMMORTALS FENYX RISING™

FROM GREAT BEGINNINGS

Script
BEN KAHN

Art
GEORGEO BROOKS

Colors
WES DZIOBA

Lettering
RICHARD STARKINGS and
COMICRAFT'S JIMMY BETANCOURT

Cover Art
GEORGEO BROOKS

DARK HORSE BOOKS

president and publisher
MIKE RICHARDSON

editor
FREDDYE MILLER

associate editor
JUDY KHUU

assistant editor
ROSE WEITZ

designer
SKYLER WEISSENFLUH

digital art technician
ANN GRAY

Neil Hankerson Executive Vice President • Tom Weddle Chief Financial Officer • Dale LaFountain Chief Information Officer • Tim Wiesch Vice President of Licensing • Matt Parkinson Vice President of Marketing • Vanessa Todd-Holmes Vice President of Production and Scheduling • Mark Bernardi Vice President of Book Trade and Digital Sales • Randy Lahrman Vice President of Product Development • Ken Lizzi General Counsel • Dave Marshall Editor in Chief • Davey Estrada Editorial Director • Chris Warner Senior Books Editor • Cary Grazzini Director of Specialty Projects • Lia Ribacchi Art Director • Matt Dryer Director of Digital Art and Prepress • Michael Gombos Senior Director of Licensed Publications • Kari Yadro Director of Custom Programs Kari Torson Director of International Licensing

SPECIAL THANKS TO JEFFREY YOHALEM, THIERRY DANSEREAU, MARIE CAUCHON, AND CAROLINE LAMACHE AT UBISOFT.

IMMORTALS FENYX RISING: FROM GREAT BEGINNINGS

Published by Dark Horse Books
A division of Dark Horse Comics LLC
10956 SE Main Street
Milwaukie, OR 97222

DarkHorse.com

To find a comics shop in your area, visit comicshoplocator.com

Library of Congress Cataloging-in-Publication Data

Names: Kahn, Ben (Comics writer), writer. | Brooks, Georgeo, artist. |
    Dzioba, Wes, colourist. | Starkings, Richard, letterer.
Title: Immortals Fenyx rising : from great beginnings / writer, Ben Kahn ;
    artist, Georgeo Brooks ; colors, Wes Dzioba ; letters, Richard Starkings
    and Comicraft.
Description: Milwaukie, OR : Dark Horse Books, 2021. | Audience: Ages 8+ |
    Audience: Grades 4-6
Identifiers: LCCN 2021010119 | ISBN 9781506719726 (trade paperback)
Subjects: LCSH: Graphic novels. | CYAC: Graphic novels. | Gods--Fiction.
Classification: LCC PZ7.7.K347 Im 2021 | DDC 741.5/973--dc23
LC record available at https://lccn.loc.gov/2021010119

First edition: November 2021
Ebook ISBN 978-1-50671-982-5
Trade Paperback ISBN 978-1-50671-972-6

1 3 5 7 9 10 8 6 4 2
Printed in China

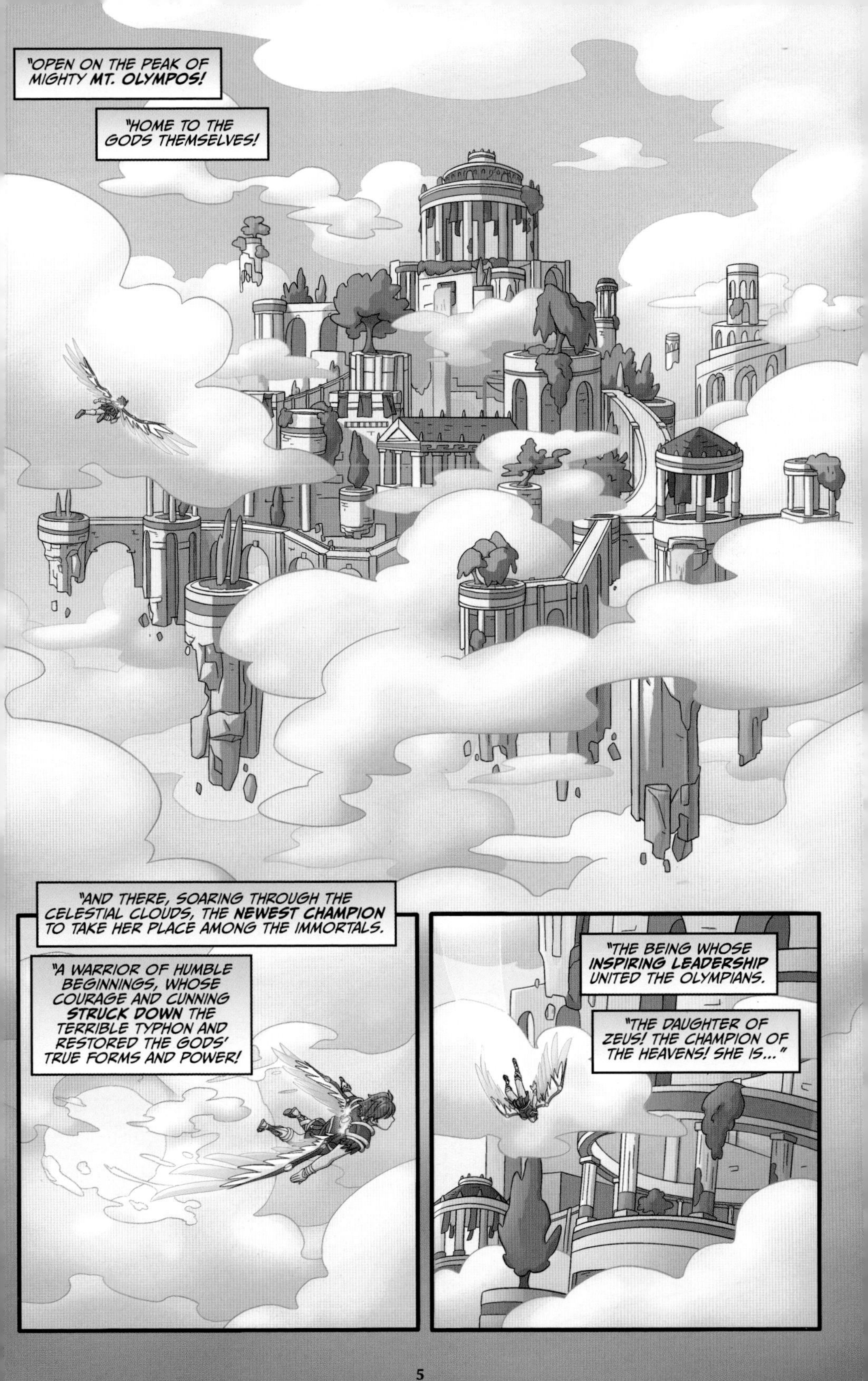
"OPEN ON THE PEAK OF MIGHTY MT. OLYMPOS!
"HOME TO THE GODS THEMSELVES!
"AND THERE, SOARING THROUGH THE CELESTIAL CLOUDS, THE NEWEST CHAMPION TO TAKE HER PLACE AMONG THE IMMORTALS.
"A WARRIOR OF HUMBLE BEGINNINGS, WHOSE COURAGE AND CUNNING STRUCK DOWN THE TERRIBLE TYPHON AND RESTORED THE GODS' TRUE FORMS AND POWER!
"THE BEING WHOSE INSPIRING LEADERSHIP UNITED THE OLYMPIANS.
"THE DAUGHTER OF ZEUS! THE CHAMPION OF THE HEAVENS! SHE IS..."

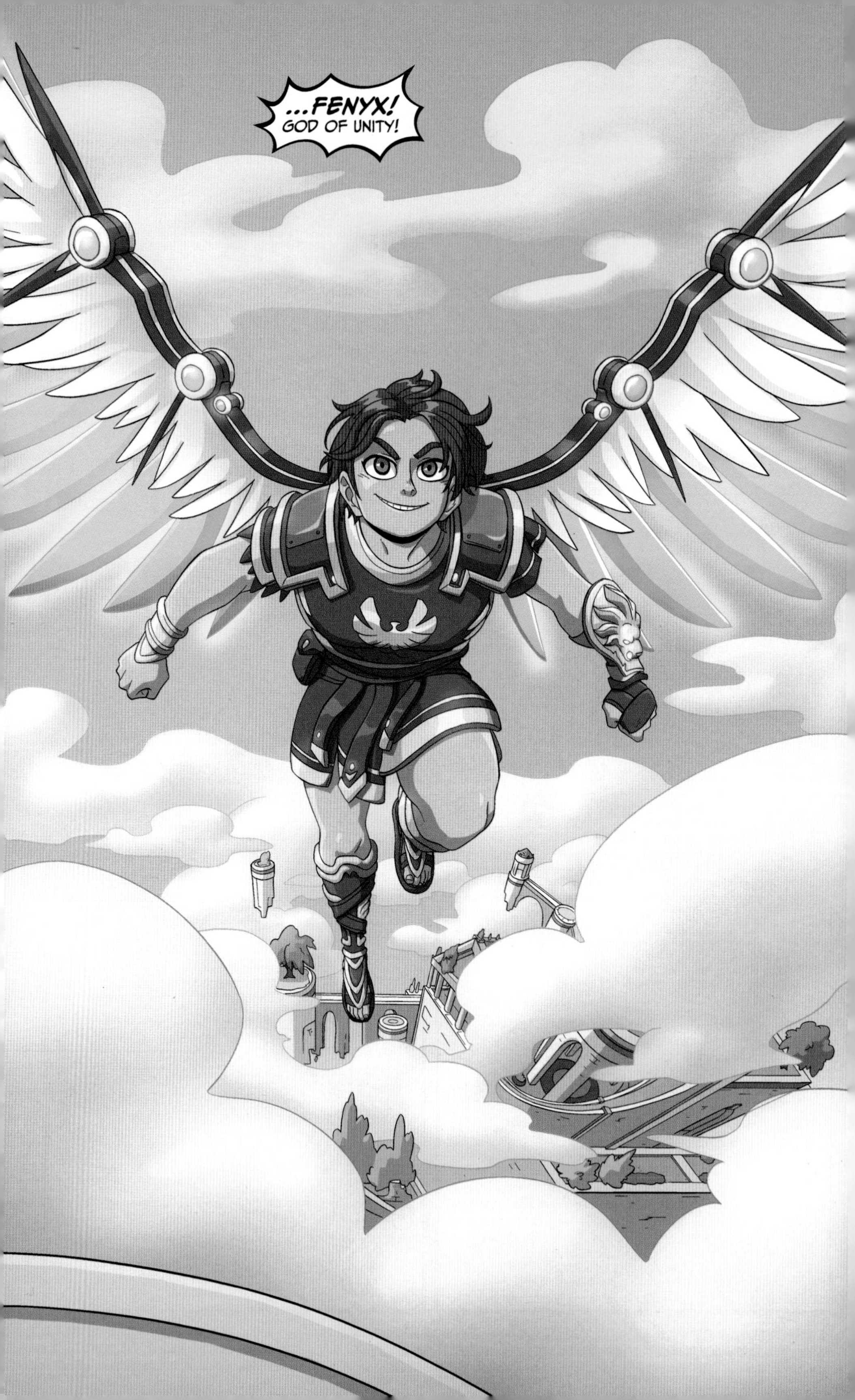
...FENYX!
GOD OF UNITY!

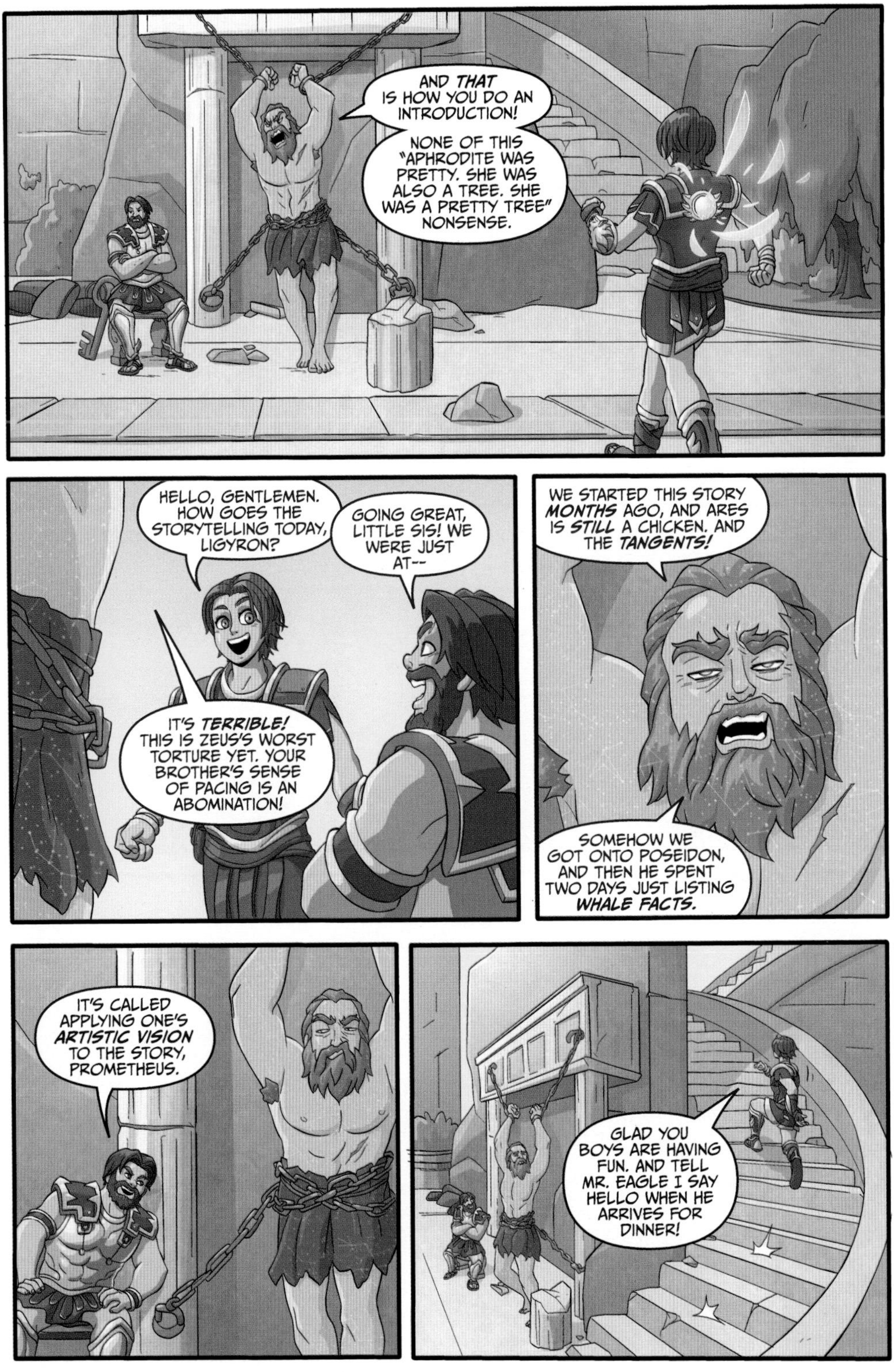
AND *THAT* IS HOW YOU DO AN INTRODUCTION!
NONE OF THIS "APHRODITE WAS PRETTY. SHE WAS ALSO A TREE. SHE WAS A PRETTY TREE" NONSENSE.
HELLO, GENTLEMEN. HOW GOES THE STORYTELLING TODAY, LIGYRON?
GOING GREAT, LITTLE SIS! WE WERE JUST AT--
IT'S *TERRIBLE!* THIS IS ZEUS'S WORST TORTURE YET. YOUR BROTHER'S SENSE OF PACING IS AN ABOMINATION!
WE STARTED THIS STORY *MONTHS* AGO, AND ARES IS *STILL* A CHICKEN. AND THE *TANGENTS!*
SOMEHOW WE GOT ONTO POSEIDON, AND THEN HE SPENT TWO DAYS JUST LISTING *WHALE FACTS.*
IT'S CALLED APPLYING ONE'S *ARTISTIC VISION* TO THE STORY, PROMETHEUS.
GLAD YOU BOYS ARE HAVING FUN. AND TELL MR. EAGLE I SAY HELLO WHEN HE ARRIVES FOR DINNER!

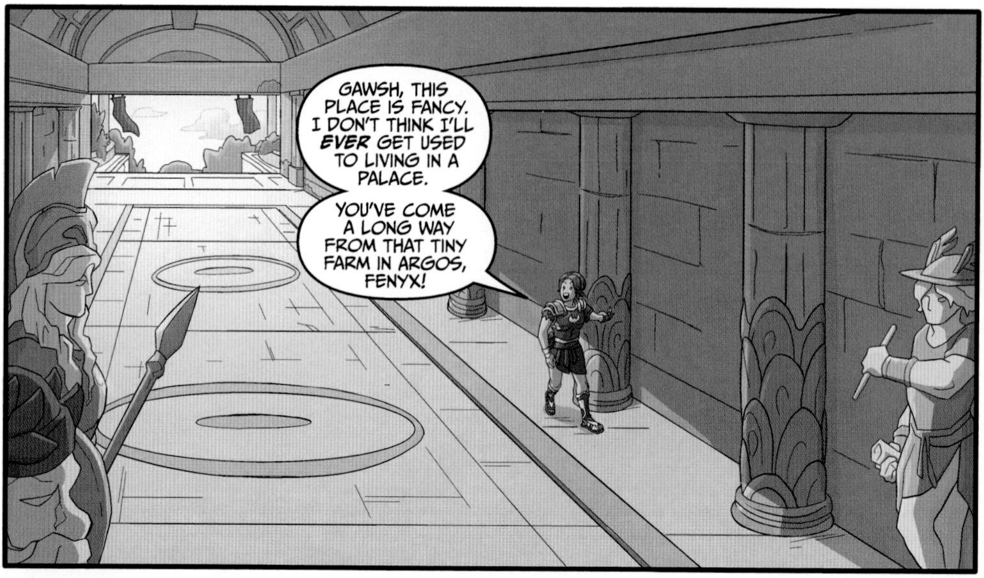
GAWSH, THIS PLACE IS FANCY. I DON'T THINK I'LL ***EVER*** GET USED TO LIVING IN A PALACE.
YOU'VE COME A LONG WAY FROM THAT TINY FARM IN ARGOS, FENYX!

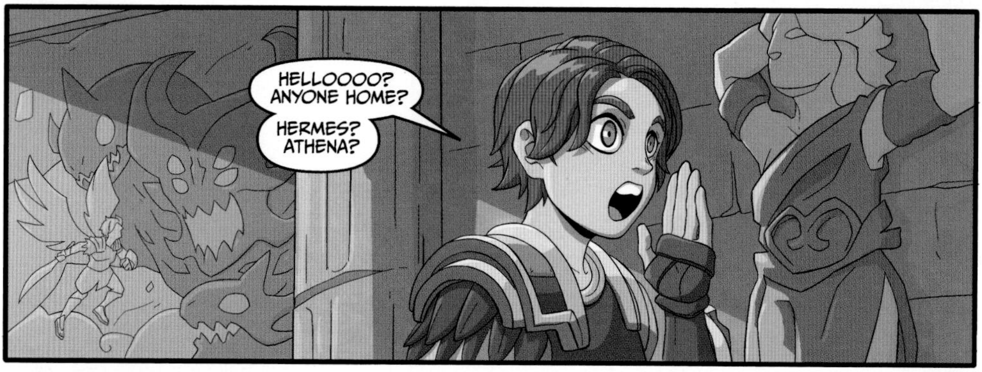
HELLOOOO? ANYONE HOME?
HERMES? ATHENA?

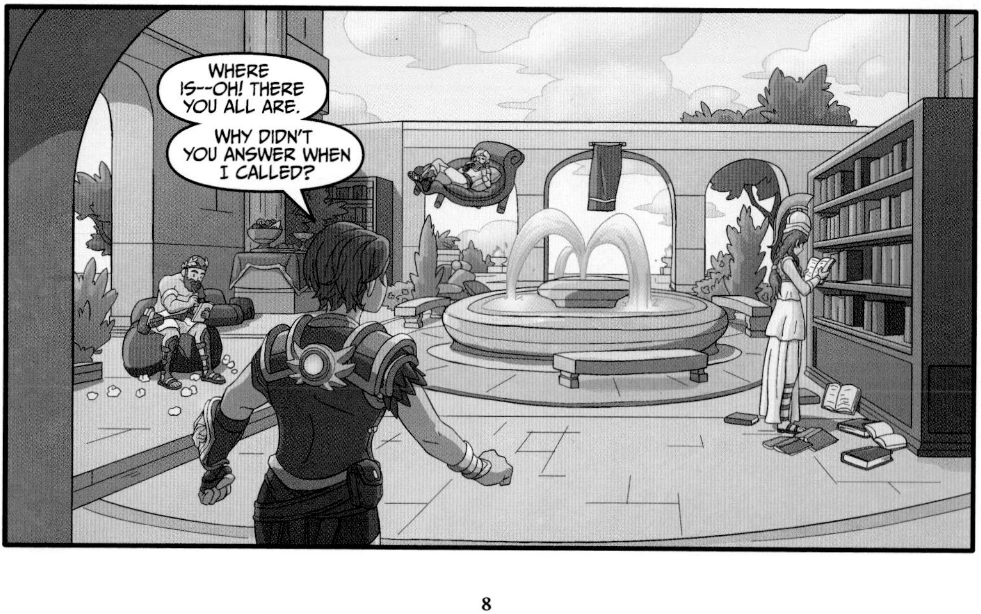
WHERE IS--OH! THERE YOU ALL ARE.
WHY DIDN'T YOU ANSWER WHEN I CALLED?

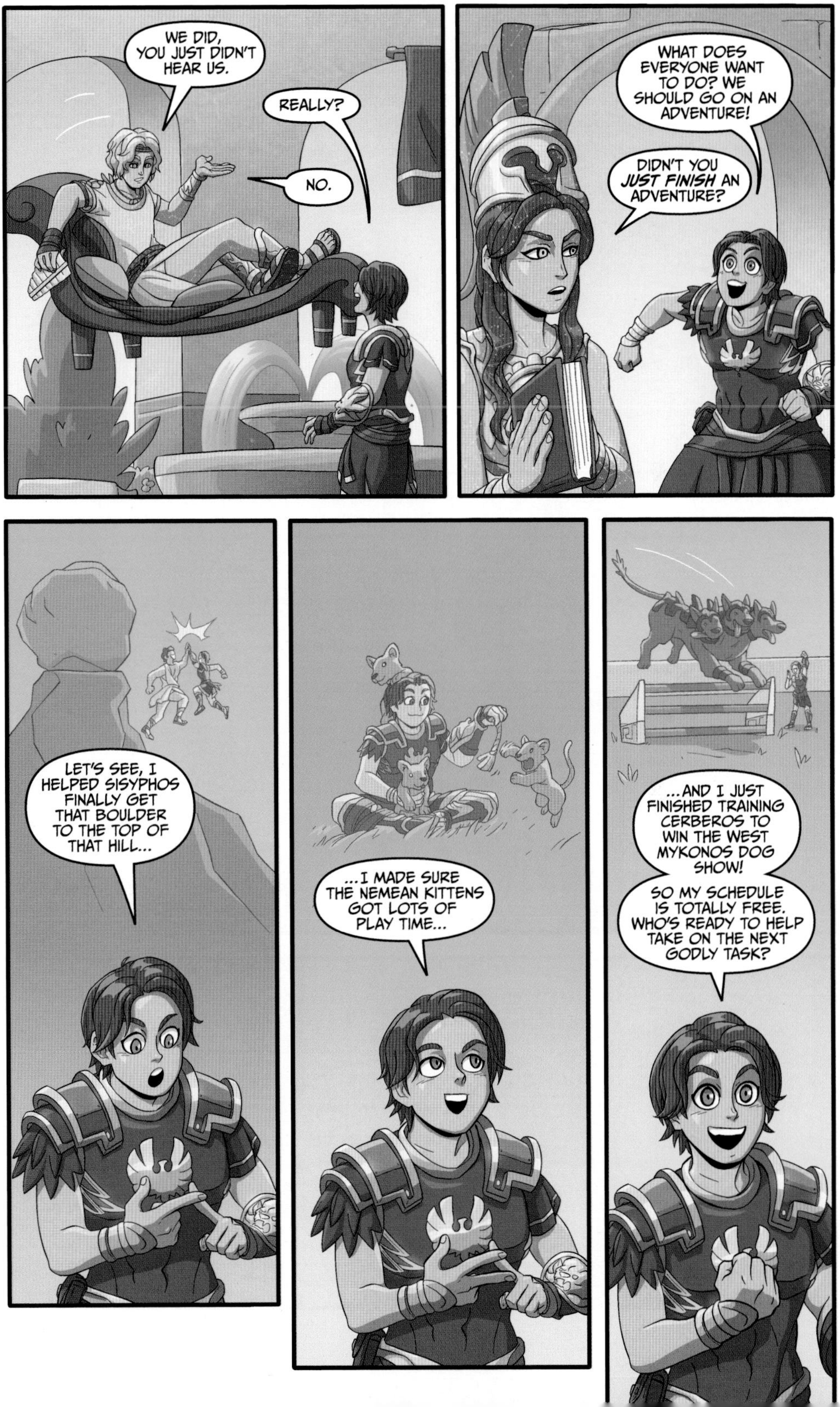
WE DID, YOU JUST DIDN'T HEAR US.
REALLY?
NO.
WHAT DOES EVERYONE WANT TO DO? WE SHOULD GO ON AN ADVENTURE!
DIDN'T YOU *JUST FINISH* AN ADVENTURE?
LET'S SEE, I HELPED SISYPHOS FINALLY GET THAT BOULDER TO THE TOP OF THAT HILL...
...I MADE SURE THE NEMEAN KITTENS GOT LOTS OF PLAY TIME...
...AND I JUST FINISHED TRAINING CERBEROS TO WIN THE WEST MYKONOS DOG SHOW!
SO MY SCHEDULE IS TOTALLY FREE. WHO'S READY TO HELP TAKE ON THE NEXT GODLY TASK?

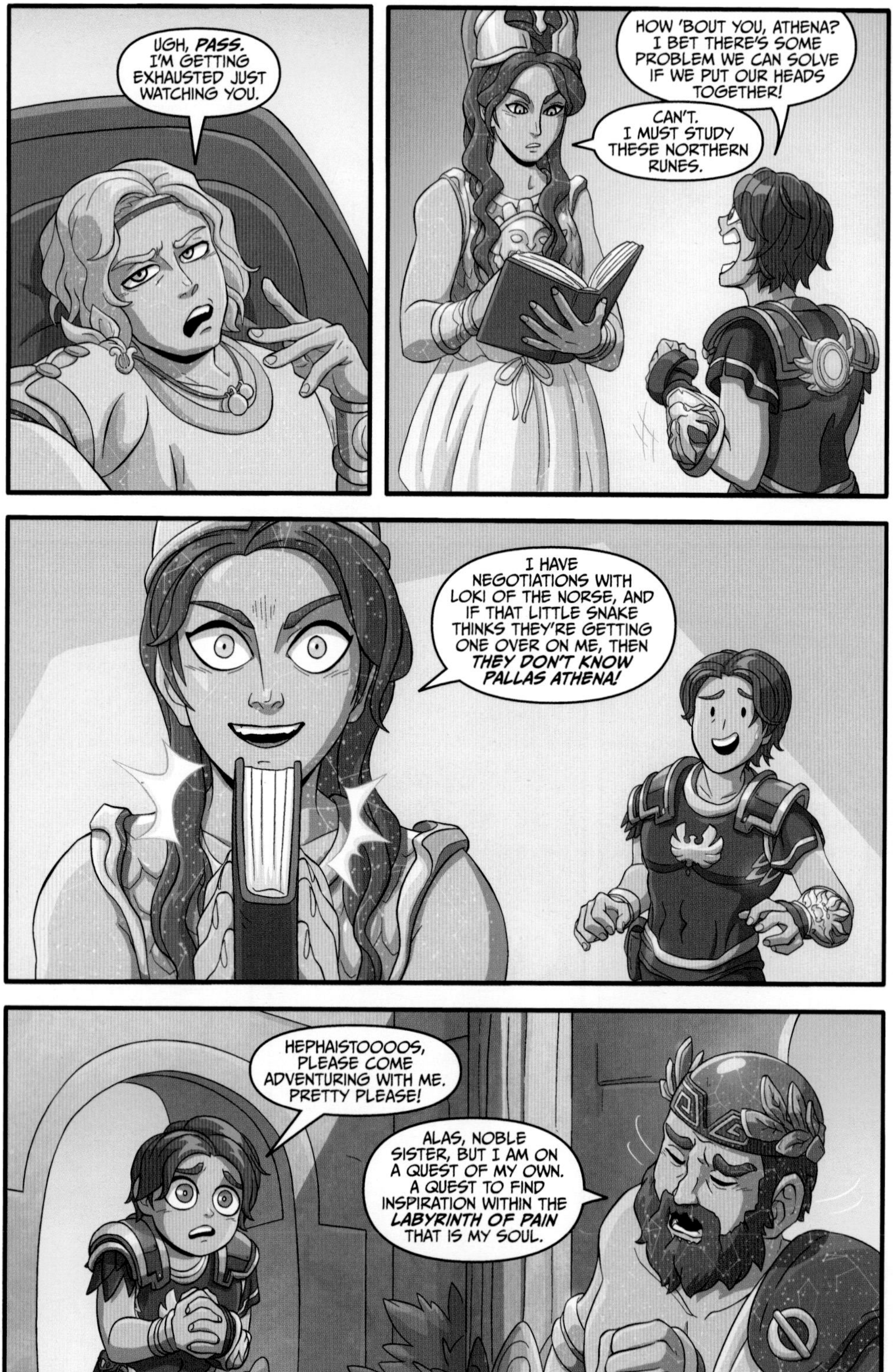
UGH, PASS. I'M GETTING EXHAUSTED JUST WATCHING YOU.
HOW 'BOUT YOU, ATHENA? I BET THERE'S SOME PROBLEM WE CAN SOLVE IF WE PUT OUR HEADS TOGETHER!
CAN'T. I MUST STUDY THESE NORTHERN RUNES.
I HAVE NEGOTIATIONS WITH LOKI OF THE NORSE, AND IF THAT LITTLE SNAKE THINKS THEY'RE GETTING ONE OVER ON ME, THEN THEY DON'T KNOW PALLAS ATHENA!
HEPHAISTOOOOS, PLEASE COME ADVENTURING WITH ME. PRETTY PLEASE!
ALAS, NOBLE SISTER, BUT I AM ON A QUEST OF MY OWN. A QUEST TO FIND INSPIRATION WITHIN THE LABYRINTH OF PAIN THAT IS MY SOUL.

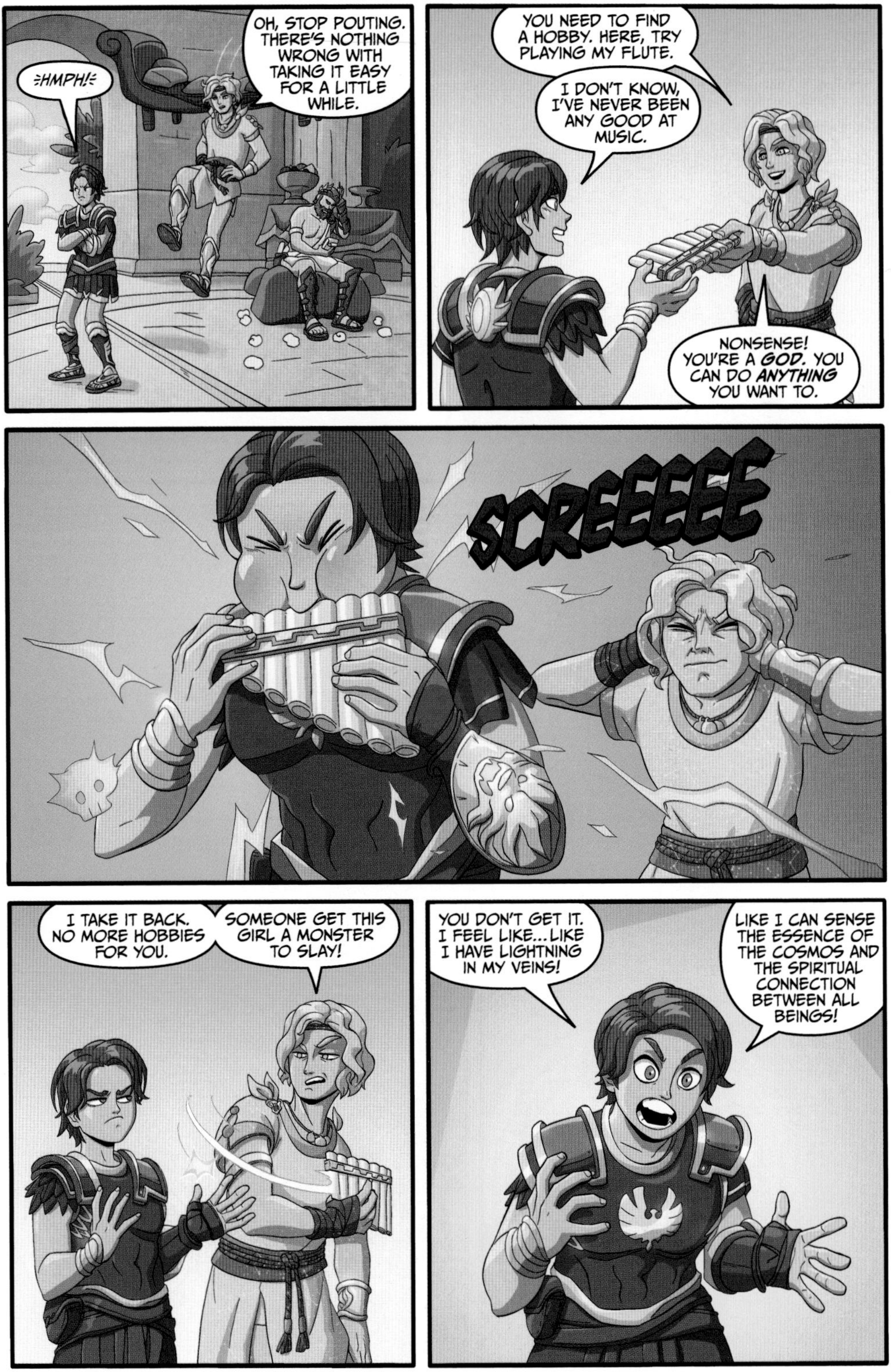

OH, STOP POUTING. THERE'S NOTHING WRONG WITH TAKING IT EASY FOR A LITTLE WHILE.
HMPH!
YOU NEED TO FIND A HOBBY. HERE, TRY PLAYING MY FLUTE.
I DON'T KNOW, I'VE NEVER BEEN ANY GOOD AT MUSIC.
NONSENSE! YOU'RE A *GOD.* YOU CAN DO *ANYTHING* YOU WANT TO.
SCREEEEEE
I TAKE IT BACK. NO MORE HOBBIES FOR YOU.
SOMEONE GET THIS GIRL A MONSTER TO SLAY!
YOU DON'T GET IT. I FEEL LIKE... LIKE I HAVE LIGHTNING IN MY VEINS!
LIKE I CAN SENSE THE ESSENCE OF THE COSMOS AND THE SPIRITUAL CONNECTION BETWEEN ALL BEINGS!

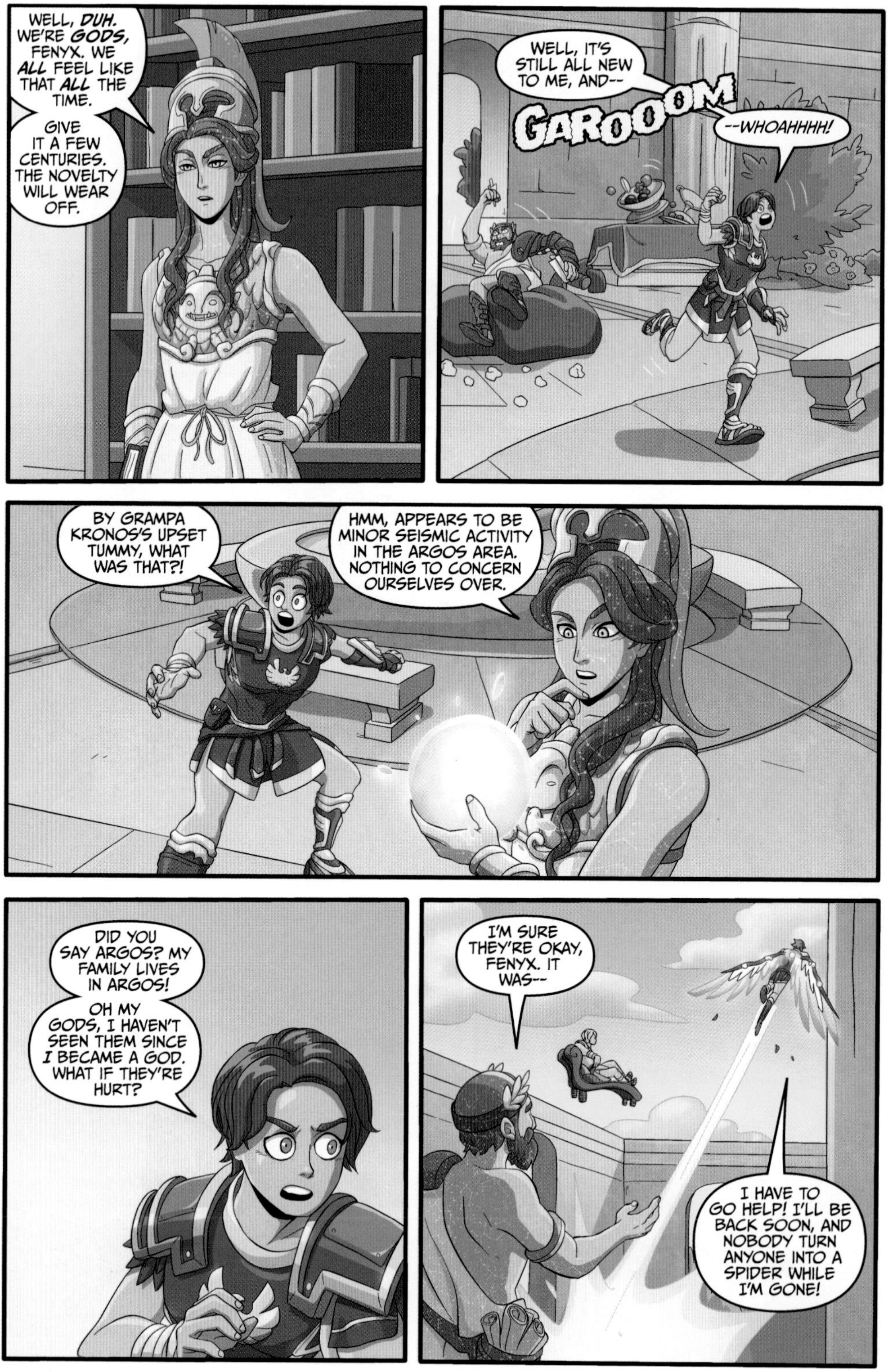
WELL, DUH. WE'RE GODS, FENYX. WE ALL FEEL LIKE THAT ALL THE TIME.
GIVE IT A FEW CENTURIES. THE NOVELTY WILL WEAR OFF.
WELL, IT'S STILL ALL NEW TO ME, AND--
GAROOOM
--WHOAHHHH!
BY GRAMPA KRONOS'S UPSET TUMMY, WHAT WAS THAT?!
HMM, APPEARS TO BE MINOR SEISMIC ACTIVITY IN THE ARGOS AREA. NOTHING TO CONCERN OURSELVES OVER.
DID YOU SAY ARGOS? MY FAMILY LIVES IN ARGOS!
OH MY GODS, I HAVEN'T SEEN THEM SINCE I BECAME A GOD. WHAT IF THEY'RE HURT?
I'M SURE THEY'RE OKAY, FENYX. IT WAS--
I HAVE TO GO HELP! I'LL BE BACK SOON, AND NOBODY TURN ANYONE INTO A SPIDER WHILE I'M GONE!

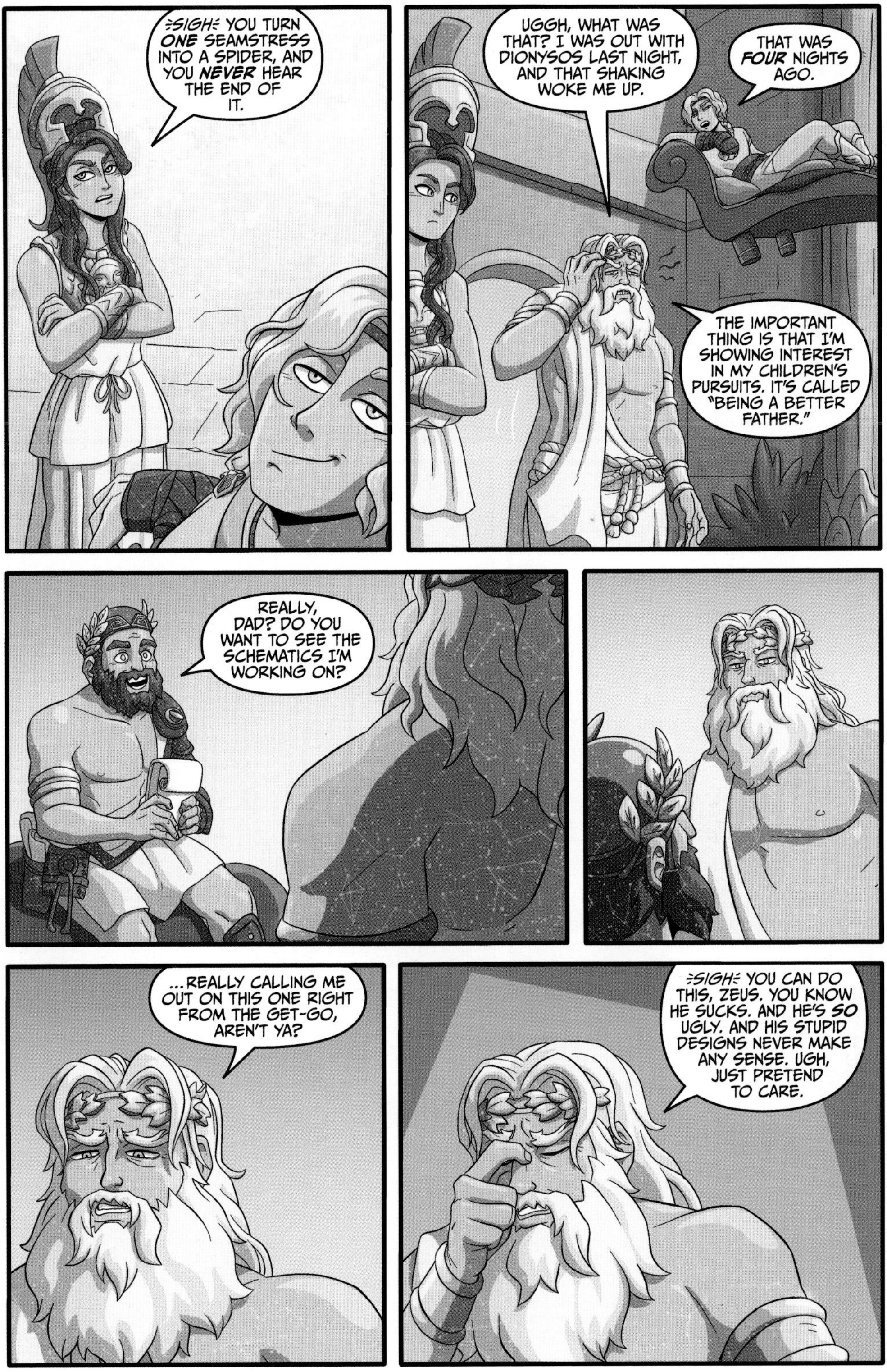

=SIGH= YOU TURN ONE SEAMSTRESS INTO A SPIDER, AND YOU NEVER HEAR THE END OF IT.
UGGH, WHAT WAS THAT? I WAS OUT WITH DIONYSOS LAST NIGHT, AND THAT SHAKING WOKE ME UP.
THAT WAS FOUR NIGHTS AGO.
THE IMPORTANT THING IS THAT I'M SHOWING INTEREST IN MY CHILDREN'S PURSUITS. IT'S CALLED "BEING A BETTER FATHER."
REALLY, DAD? DO YOU WANT TO SEE THE SCHEMATICS I'M WORKING ON?
...REALLY CALLING ME OUT ON THIS ONE RIGHT FROM THE GET-GO, AREN'T YA?
=SIGH= YOU CAN DO THIS, ZEUS. YOU KNOW HE SUCKS. AND HE'S SO UGLY. AND HIS STUPID DESIGNS NEVER MAKE ANY SENSE. UGH, JUST PRETEND TO CARE.

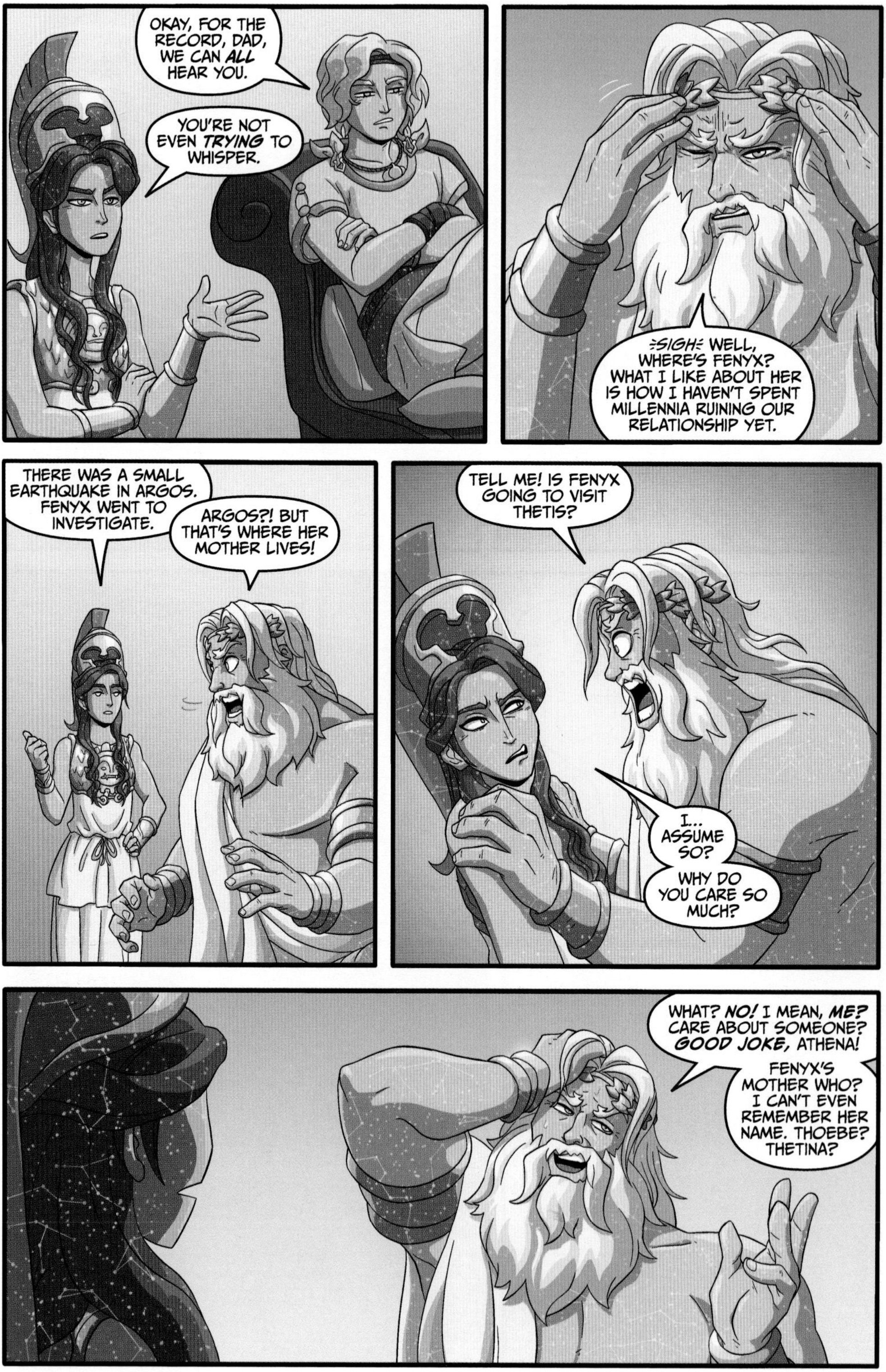
OKAY, FOR THE RECORD, DAD, WE CAN ALL HEAR YOU.
YOU'RE NOT EVEN TRYING TO WHISPER.
SIGH WELL, WHERE'S FENYX? WHAT I LIKE ABOUT HER IS HOW I HAVEN'T SPENT MILLENNIA RUINING OUR RELATIONSHIP YET.
THERE WAS A SMALL EARTHQUAKE IN ARGOS. FENYX WENT TO INVESTIGATE.
ARGOS?! BUT THAT'S WHERE HER MOTHER LIVES!
TELL ME! IS FENYX GOING TO VISIT THETIS?
I... ASSUME SO?
WHY DO YOU CARE SO MUCH?
WHAT? NO! I MEAN, ME? CARE ABOUT SOMEONE? GOOD JOKE, ATHENA!
FENYX'S MOTHER WHO? I CAN'T EVEN REMEMBER HER NAME. THOEBE? THETINA?

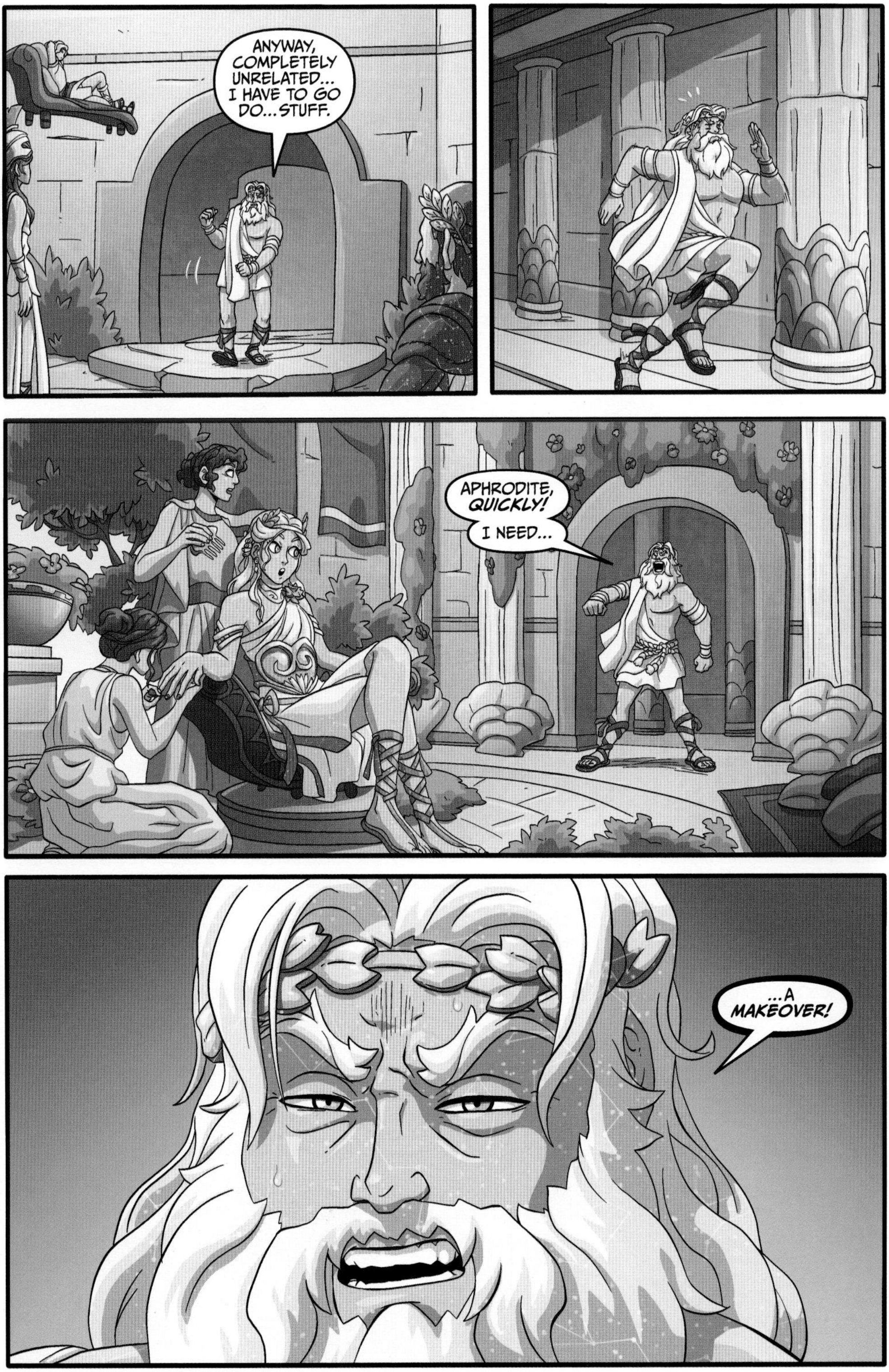
ANYWAY, COMPLETELY UNRELATED... I HAVE TO GO DO...STUFF.
APHRODITE, QUICKLY!
I NEED...
...A MAKEOVER!

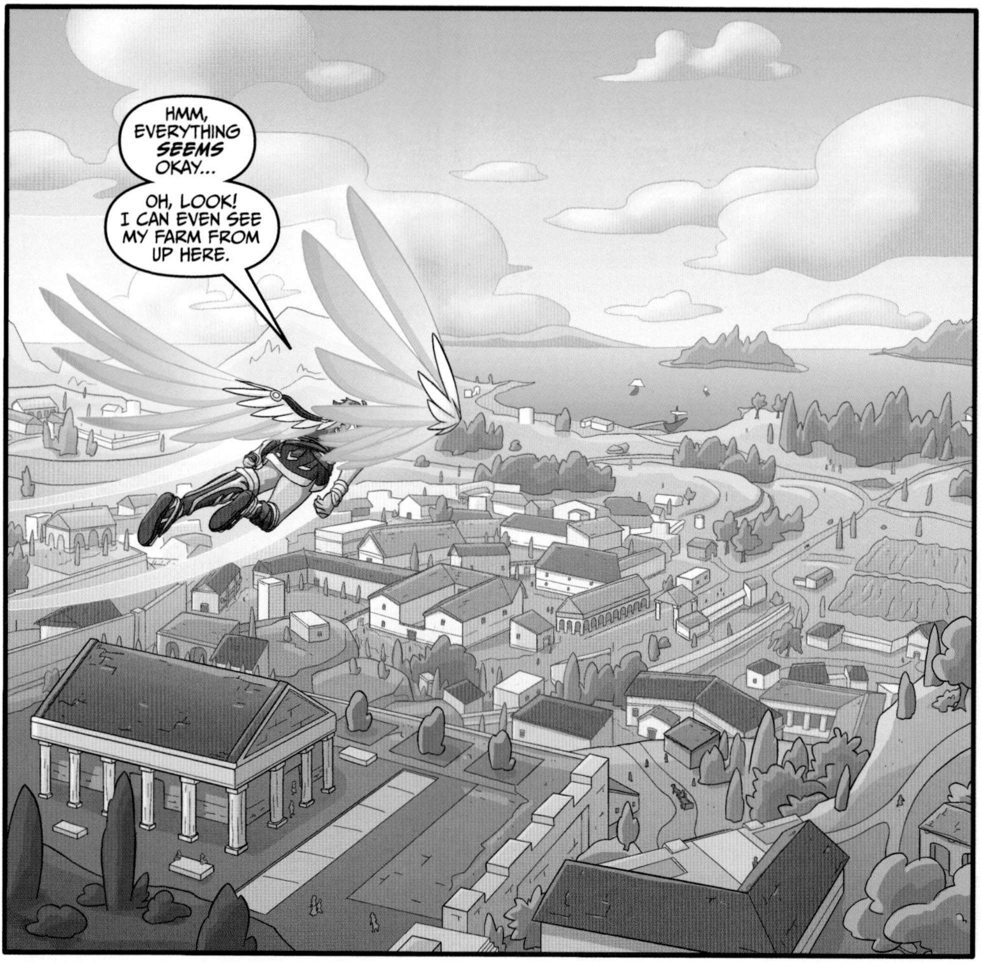
HMM, EVERYTHING SEEMS OKAY...
OH, LOOK! I CAN EVEN SEE MY FARM FROM UP HERE.

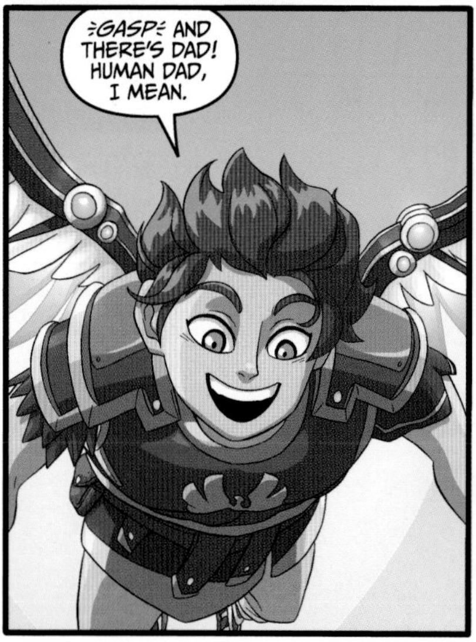
=GASP= AND THERE'S DAD! HUMAN DAD, I MEAN.

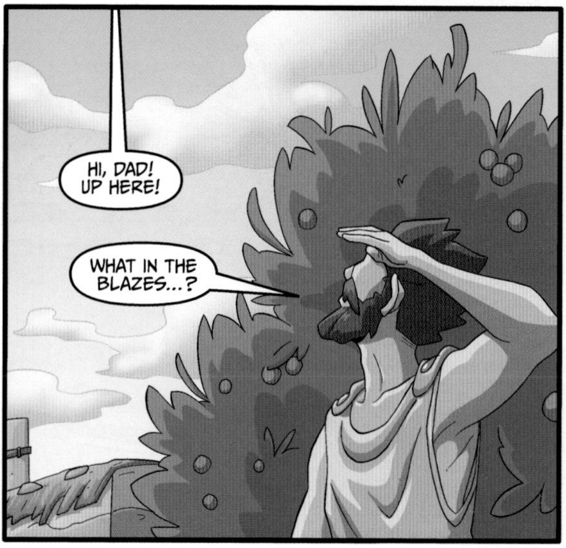
HI, DAD! UP HERE!
WHAT IN THE BLAZES...?

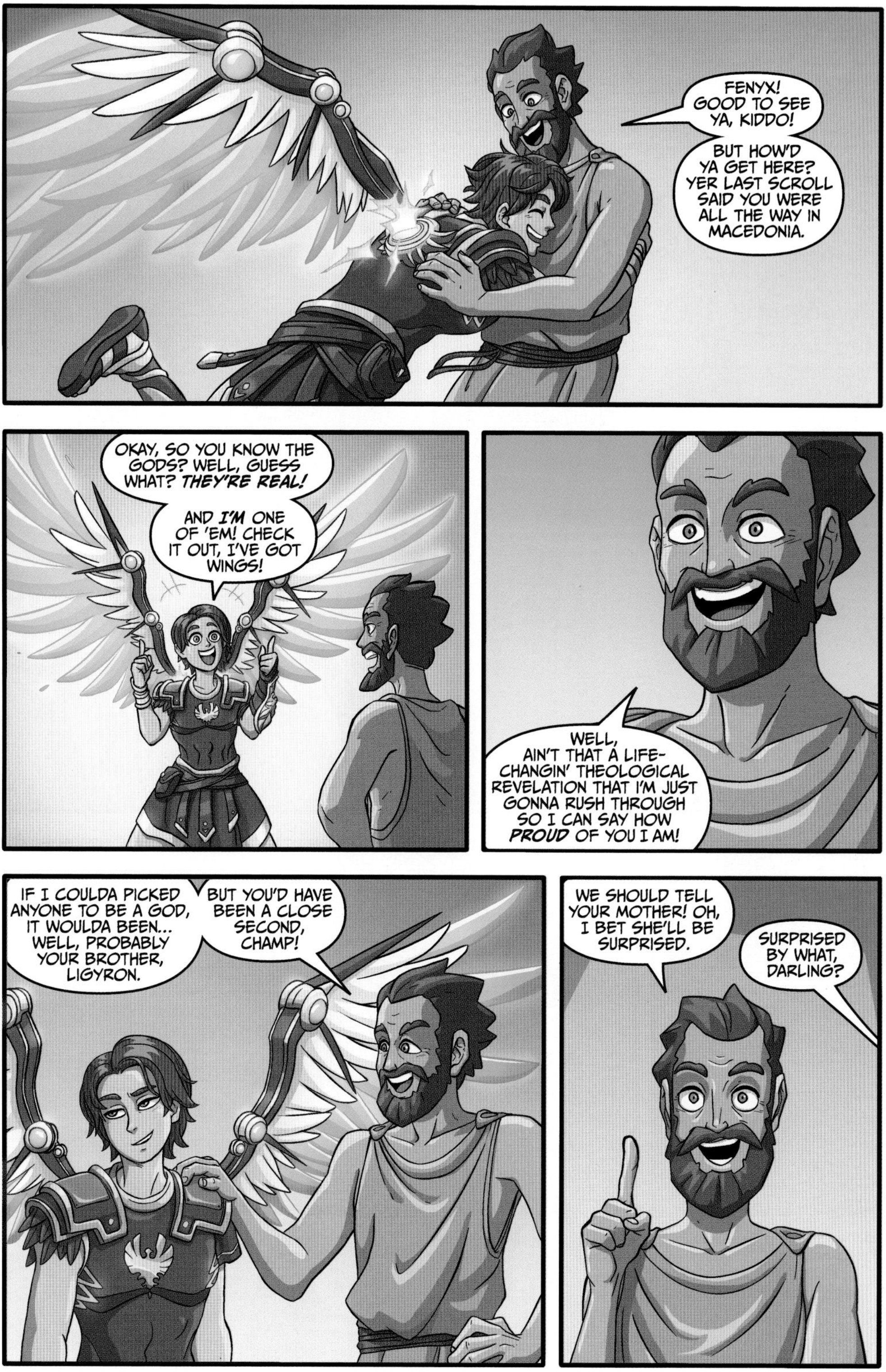
FENYX! GOOD TO SEE YA, KIDDO!
BUT HOW'D YA GET HERE? YER LAST SCROLL SAID YOU WERE ALL THE WAY IN MACEDONIA.
OKAY, SO YOU KNOW THE GODS? WELL, GUESS WHAT? *THEY'RE REAL!*
AND *I'M* ONE OF 'EM! CHECK IT OUT, I'VE GOT WINGS!
WELL, AIN'T THAT A LIFE-CHANGIN' THEOLOGICAL REVELATION THAT I'M JUST GONNA RUSH THROUGH SO I CAN SAY HOW *PROUD* OF YOU I AM!
IF I COULDA PICKED ANYONE TO BE A GOD, IT WOULDA BEEN... WELL, PROBABLY YOUR BROTHER, LIGYRON.
BUT YOU'D HAVE BEEN A CLOSE SECOND, CHAMP!
WE SHOULD TELL YOUR MOTHER! OH, I BET SHE'LL BE SURPRISED.
SURPRISED BY WHAT, DARLING?

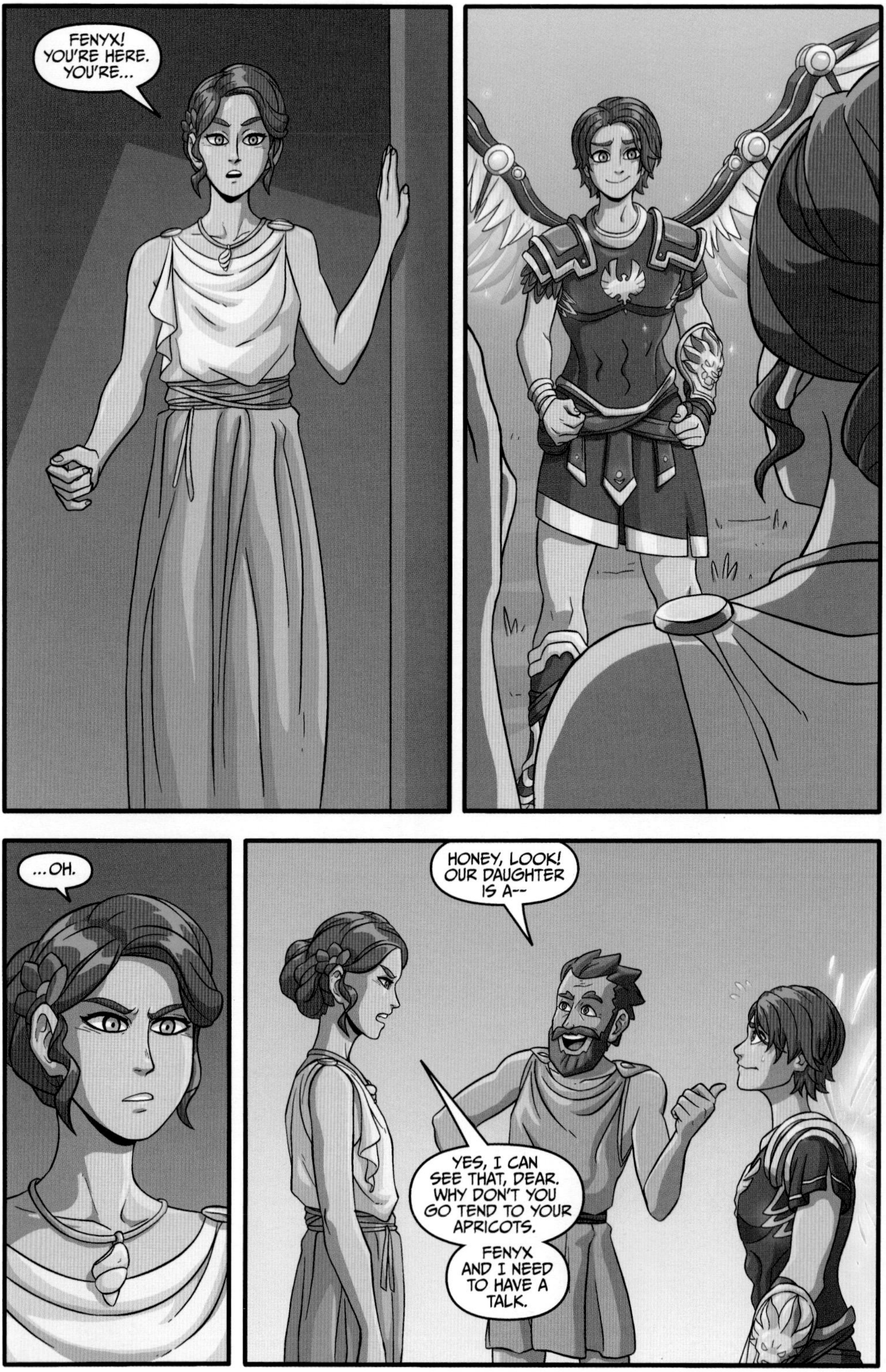
FENYX! YOU'RE HERE. YOU'RE...
...OH.
HONEY, LOOK! OUR DAUGHTER IS A--
YES, I CAN SEE THAT, DEAR. WHY DON'T YOU GO TEND TO YOUR APRICOTS.
FENYX AND I NEED TO HAVE A TALK.

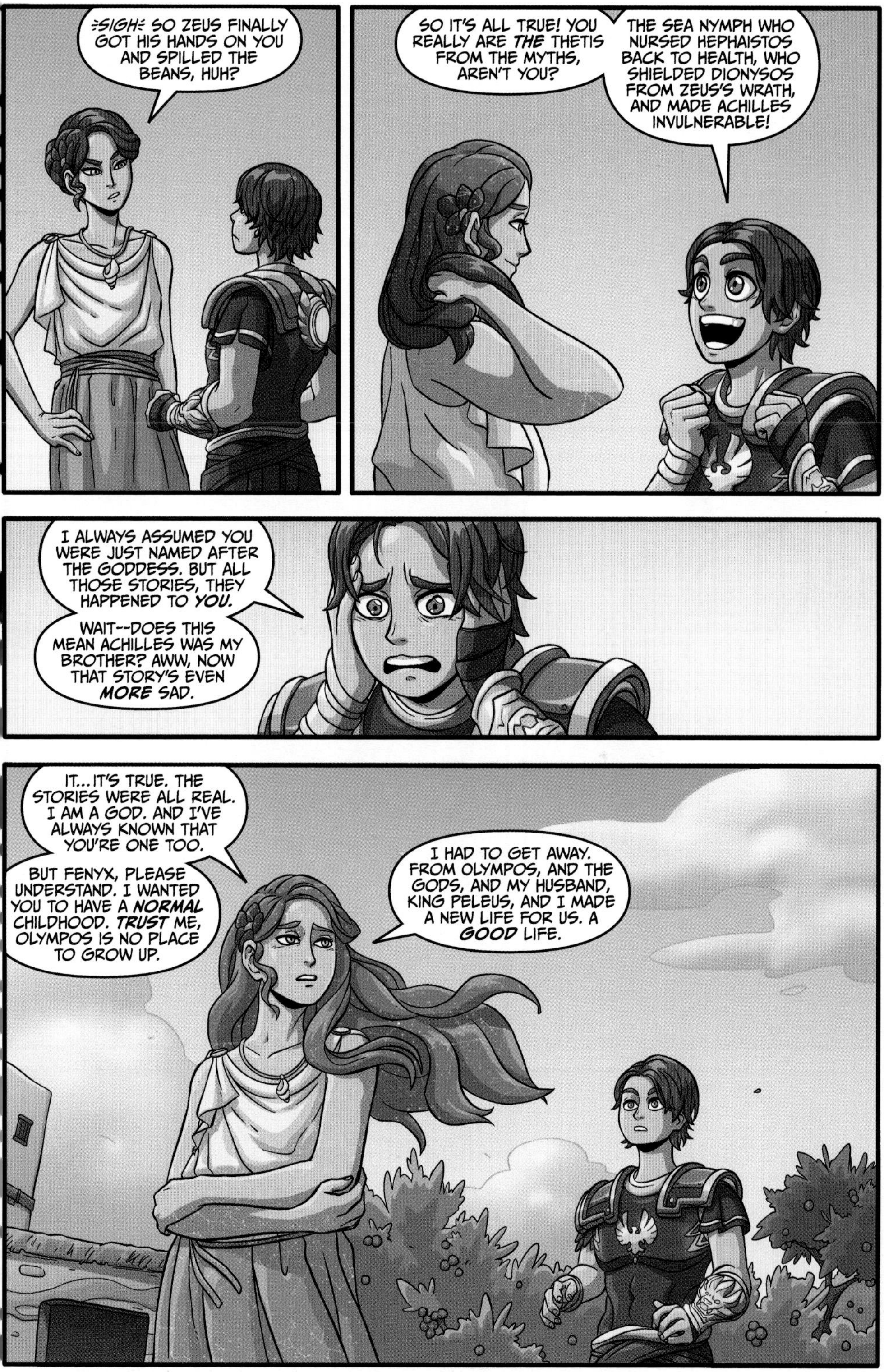

=SIGH= SO ZEUS FINALLY GOT HIS HANDS ON YOU AND SPILLED THE BEANS, HUH?
SO IT'S ALL TRUE! YOU REALLY ARE THE THETIS FROM THE MYTHS, AREN'T YOU?
THE SEA NYMPH WHO NURSED HEPHAISTOS BACK TO HEALTH, WHO SHIELDED DIONYSOS FROM ZEUS'S WRATH, AND MADE ACHILLES INVULNERABLE!
I ALWAYS ASSUMED YOU WERE JUST NAMED AFTER THE GODDESS. BUT ALL THOSE STORIES, THEY HAPPENED TO YOU.
WAIT--DOES THIS MEAN ACHILLES WAS MY BROTHER? AWW, NOW THAT STORY'S EVEN MORE SAD.
IT... IT'S TRUE. THE STORIES WERE ALL REAL. I AM A GOD. AND I'VE ALWAYS KNOWN THAT YOU'RE ONE TOO.
BUT FENYX, PLEASE UNDERSTAND. I WANTED YOU TO HAVE A NORMAL CHILDHOOD. TRUST ME, OLYMPOS IS NO PLACE TO GROW UP.
I HAD TO GET AWAY. FROM OLYMPOS, AND THE GODS, AND MY HUSBAND, KING PELEUS, AND I MADE A NEW LIFE FOR US. A GOOD LIFE.

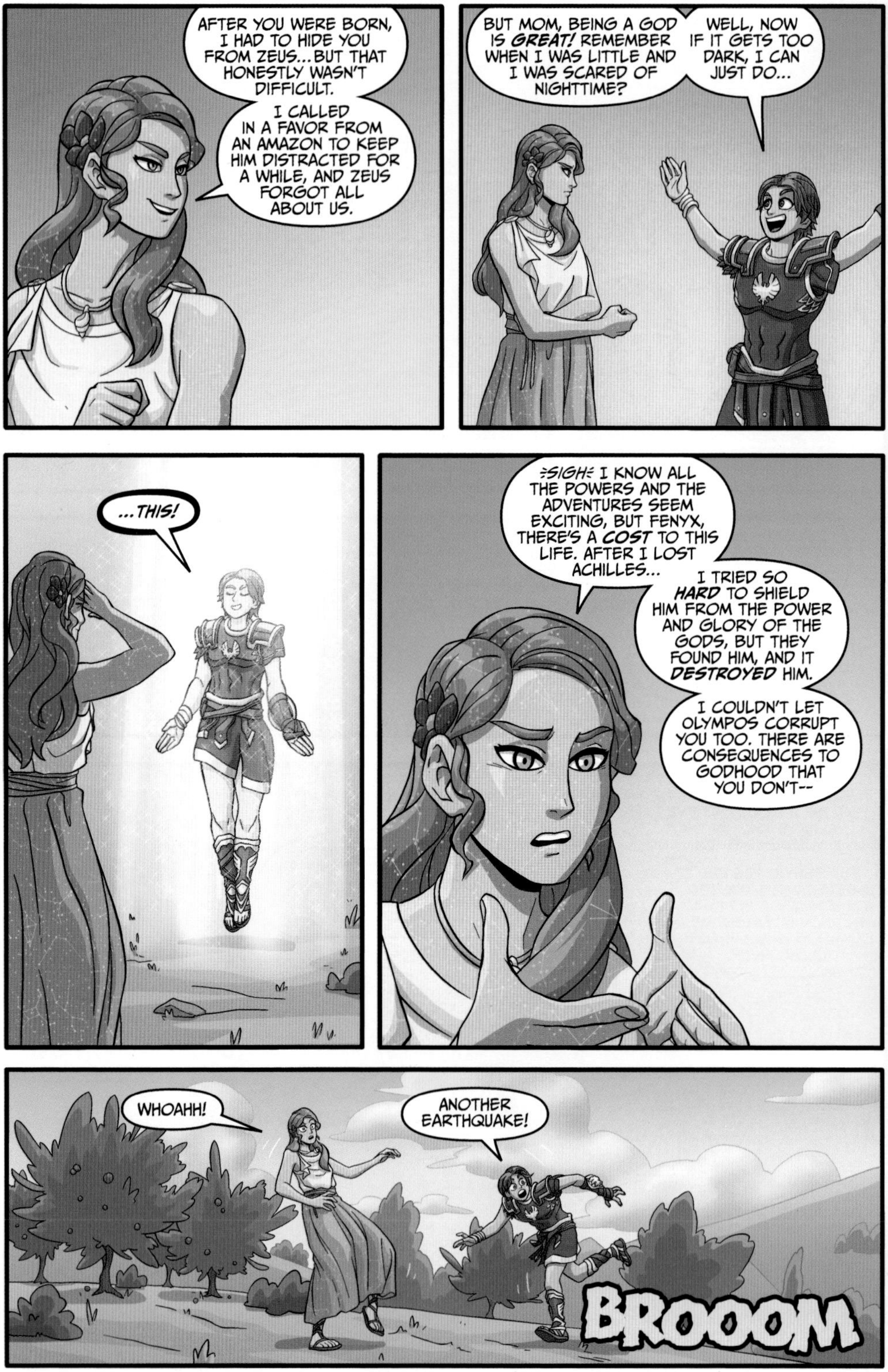
AFTER YOU WERE BORN, I HAD TO HIDE YOU FROM ZEUS...BUT THAT HONESTLY WASN'T DIFFICULT.
I CALLED IN A FAVOR FROM AN AMAZON TO KEEP HIM DISTRACTED FOR A WHILE, AND ZEUS FORGOT ALL ABOUT US.
BUT MOM, BEING A GOD IS GREAT! REMEMBER WHEN I WAS LITTLE AND I WAS SCARED OF NIGHTTIME?
WELL, NOW IF IT GETS TOO DARK, I CAN JUST DO...
...THIS!
SIGH I KNOW ALL THE POWERS AND THE ADVENTURES SEEM EXCITING, BUT FENYX, THERE'S A COST TO THIS LIFE. AFTER I LOST ACHILLES...
I TRIED SO HARD TO SHIELD HIM FROM THE POWER AND GLORY OF THE GODS, BUT THEY FOUND HIM, AND IT DESTROYED HIM.
I COULDN'T LET OLYMPOS CORRUPT YOU TOO. THERE ARE CONSEQUENCES TO GODHOOD THAT YOU DON'T--
WHOAHH!
ANOTHER EARTHQUAKE!
BROOOM

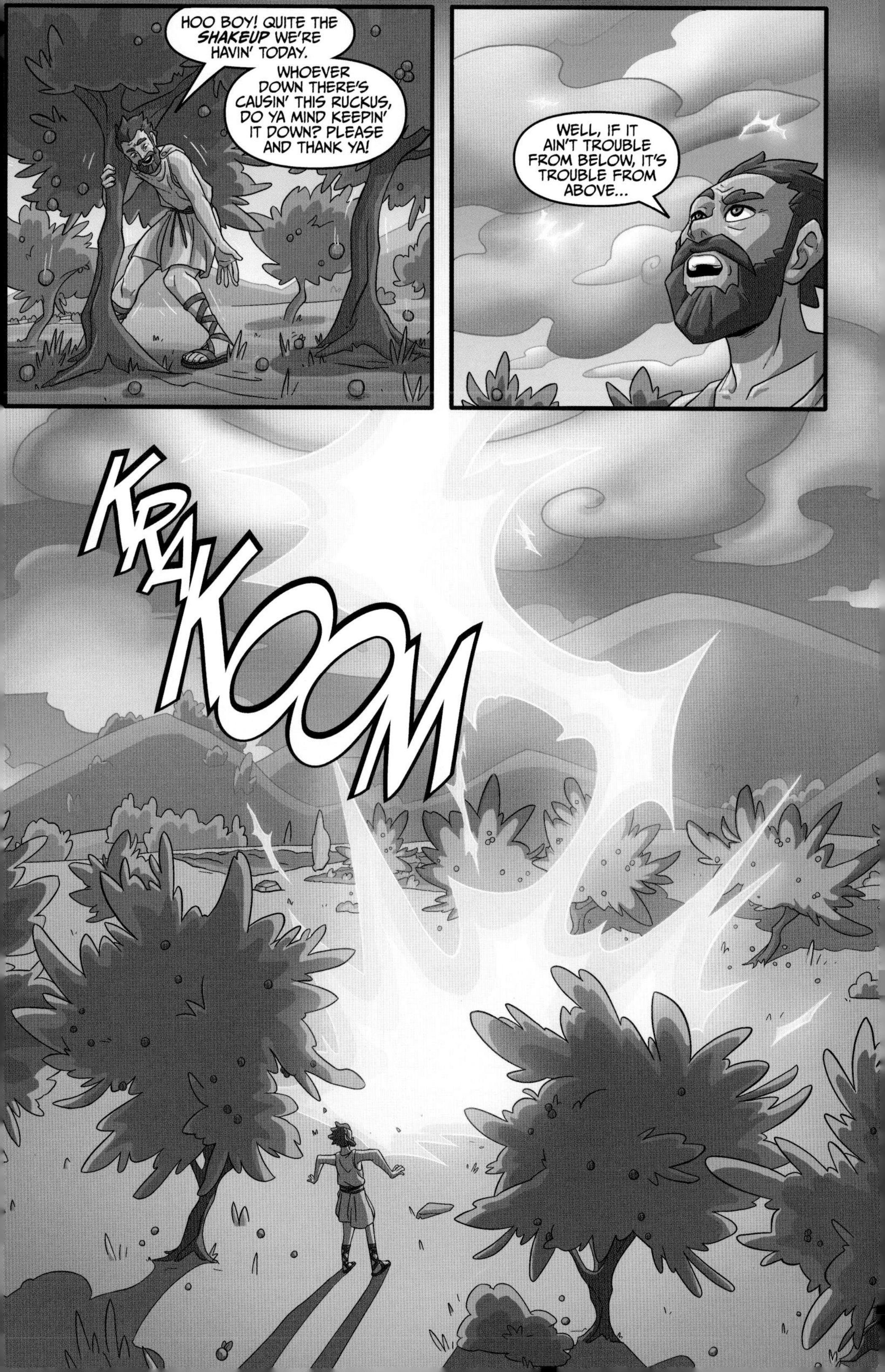
HOO BOY! QUITE THE *SHAKEUP* WE'RE HAVIN' TODAY.
WHOEVER DOWN THERE'S CAUSIN' THIS RUCKUS, DO YA MIND KEEPIN' IT DOWN? PLEASE AND THANK YA!
WELL, IF IT AIN'T TROUBLE FROM BELOW, IT'S TROUBLE FROM ABOVE...
KRAKOOM

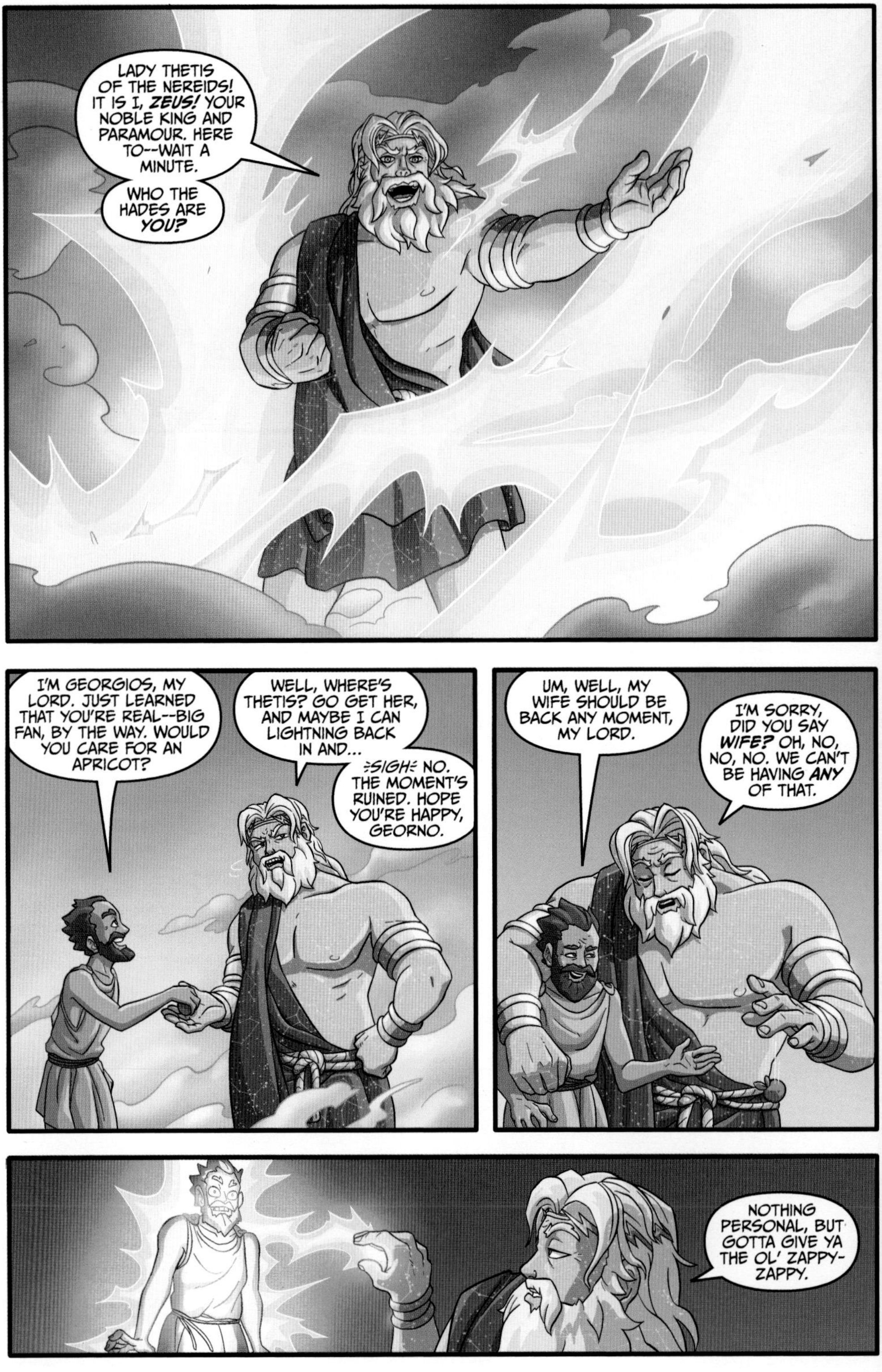
LADY THETIS OF THE NEREIDS! IT IS I, ZEUS! YOUR NOBLE KING AND PARAMOUR. HERE TO--WAIT A MINUTE.
WHO THE HADES ARE YOU?
I'M GEORGIOS, MY LORD. JUST LEARNED THAT YOU'RE REAL--BIG FAN, BY THE WAY. WOULD YOU CARE FOR AN APRICOT?
WELL, WHERE'S THETIS? GO GET HER, AND MAYBE I CAN LIGHTNING BACK IN AND...
SIGH NO. THE MOMENT'S RUINED. HOPE YOU'RE HAPPY, GEORNO.
UM, WELL, MY WIFE SHOULD BE BACK ANY MOMENT, MY LORD.
I'M SORRY, DID YOU SAY WIFE? OH, NO, NO, NO. WE CAN'T BE HAVING ANY OF THAT.
NOTHING PERSONAL, BUT GOTTA GIVE YA THE OL' ZAPPY-ZAPPY.

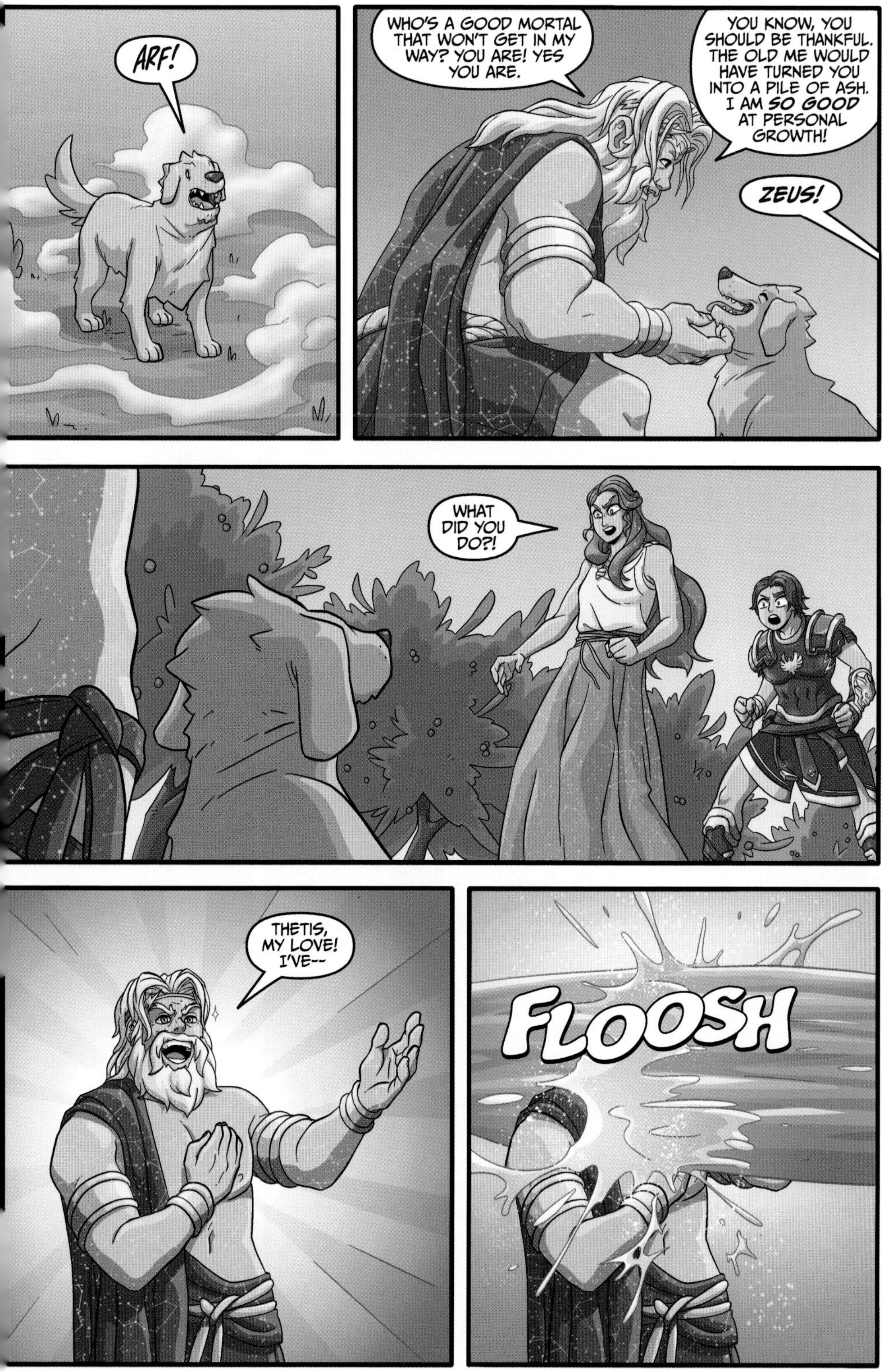
ARF!
WHO'S A GOOD MORTAL THAT WON'T GET IN MY WAY? YOU ARE! YES YOU ARE.
YOU KNOW, YOU SHOULD BE THANKFUL. THE OLD ME WOULD HAVE TURNED YOU INTO A PILE OF ASH. I AM SO GOOD AT PERSONAL GROWTH!
ZEUS!
WHAT DID YOU DO?!
THETIS, MY LOVE! I'VE--
FLOOSH

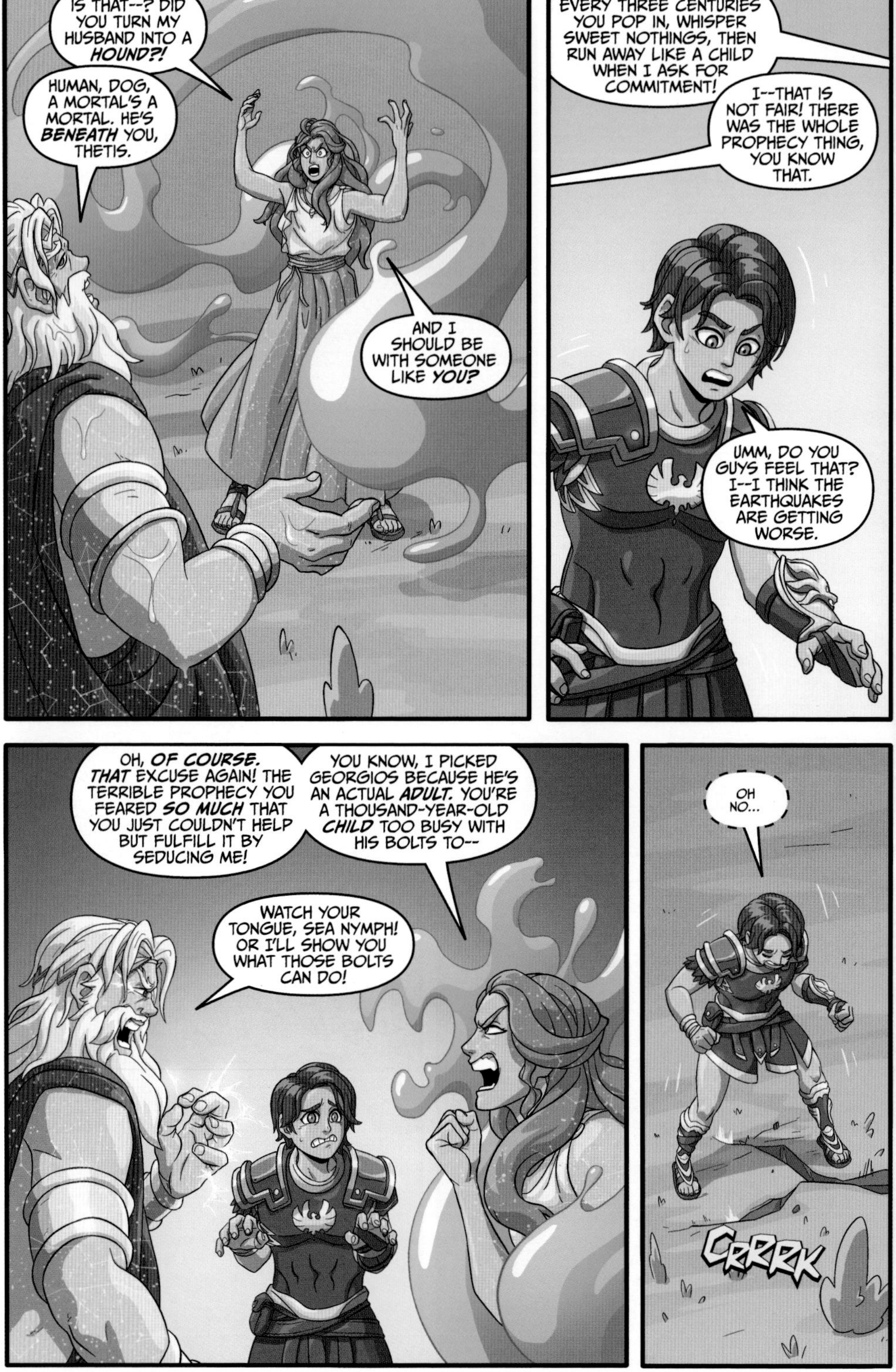
IS THAT--? DID YOU TURN MY HUSBAND INTO A ***HOUND?!***
HUMAN, DOG, A MORTAL'S A MORTAL. HE'S ***BENEATH*** YOU, THETIS.
AND I SHOULD BE WITH SOMEONE LIKE ***YOU?***
EVERY THREE CENTURIES YOU POP IN, WHISPER SWEET NOTHINGS, THEN RUN AWAY LIKE A CHILD WHEN I ASK FOR COMMITMENT!
I--THAT IS NOT FAIR! THERE WAS THE WHOLE PROPHECY THING, YOU KNOW THAT.
UMM, DO YOU GUYS FEEL THAT? I--I THINK THE EARTHQUAKES ARE GETTING WORSE.
OH, ***OF COURSE. THAT*** EXCUSE AGAIN! THE TERRIBLE PROPHECY YOU FEARED ***SO MUCH*** THAT YOU JUST COULDN'T HELP BUT FULFILL IT BY SEDUCING ME!
YOU KNOW, I PICKED GEORGIOS BECAUSE HE'S AN ACTUAL ***ADULT.*** YOU'RE A THOUSAND-YEAR-OLD ***CHILD*** TOO BUSY WITH HIS BOLTS TO--
WATCH YOUR TONGUE, SEA NYMPH! OR I'LL SHOW YOU WHAT THOSE BOLTS CAN DO!
OH NO...
CRRRK

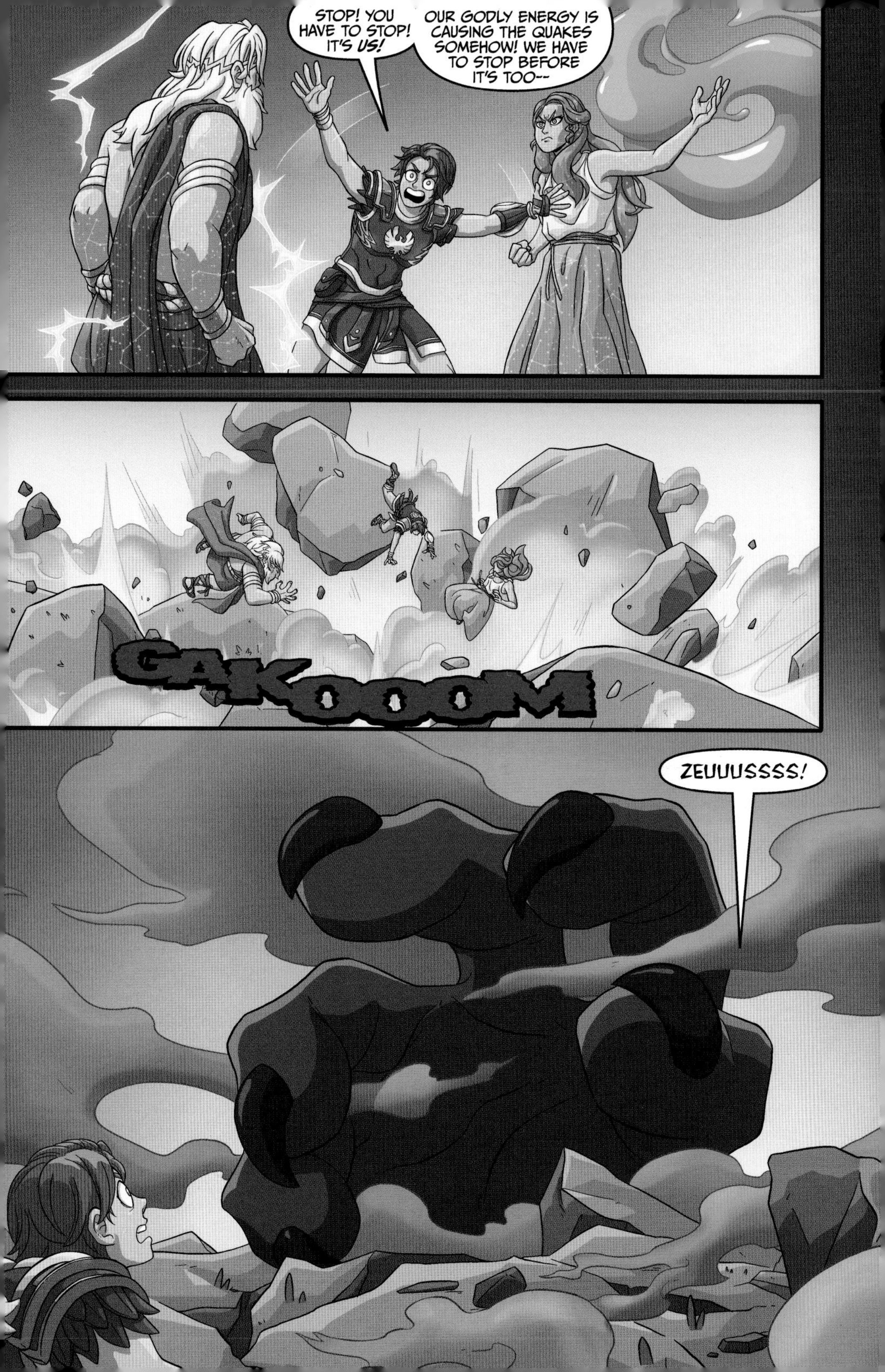
STOP! YOU HAVE TO STOP! IT'S US!
OUR GODLY ENERGY IS CAUSING THE QUAKES SOMEHOW! WE HAVE TO STOP BEFORE IT'S TOO--
GAKOOOM
ZEUUUSSSS!

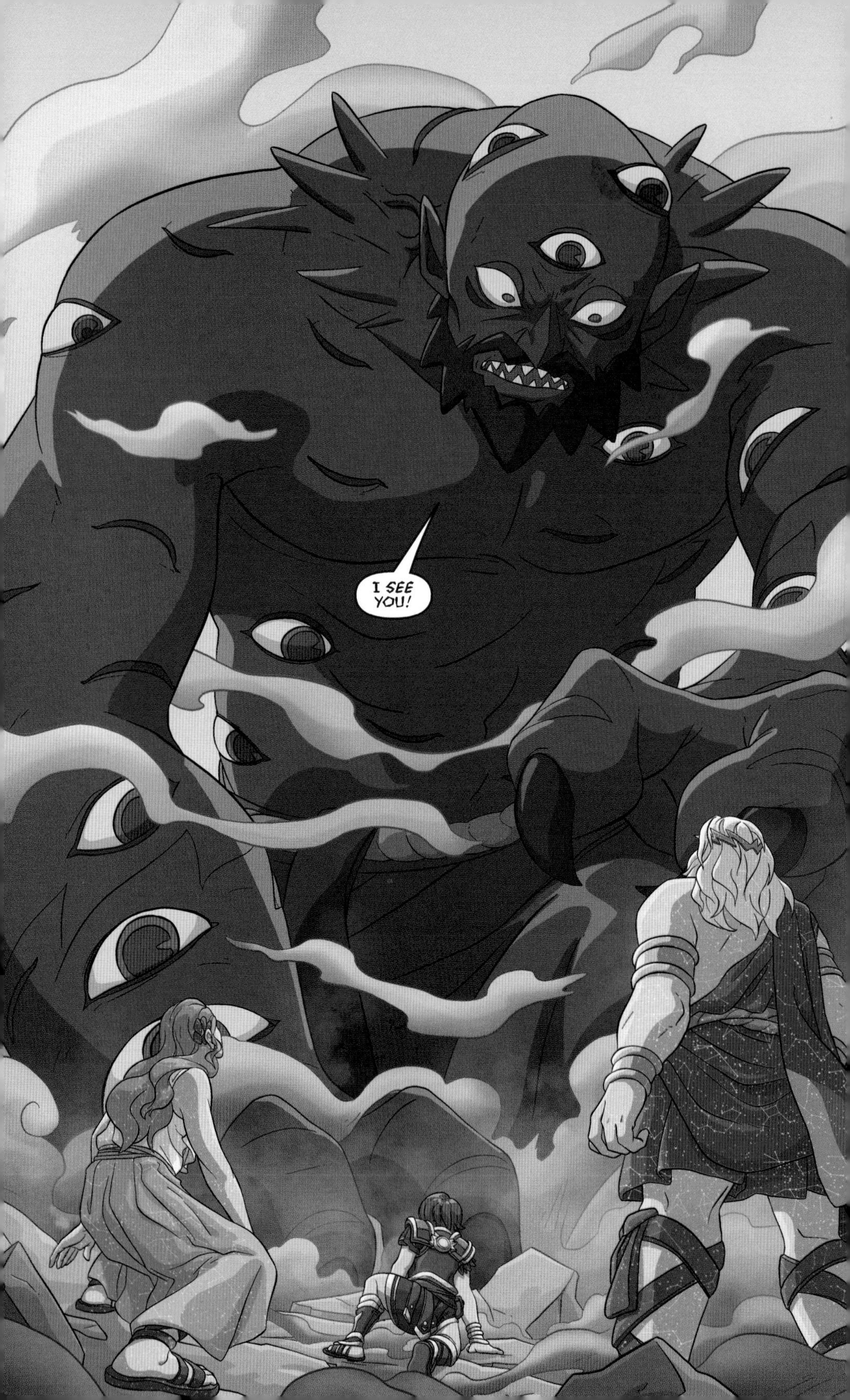
I SEE YOU!

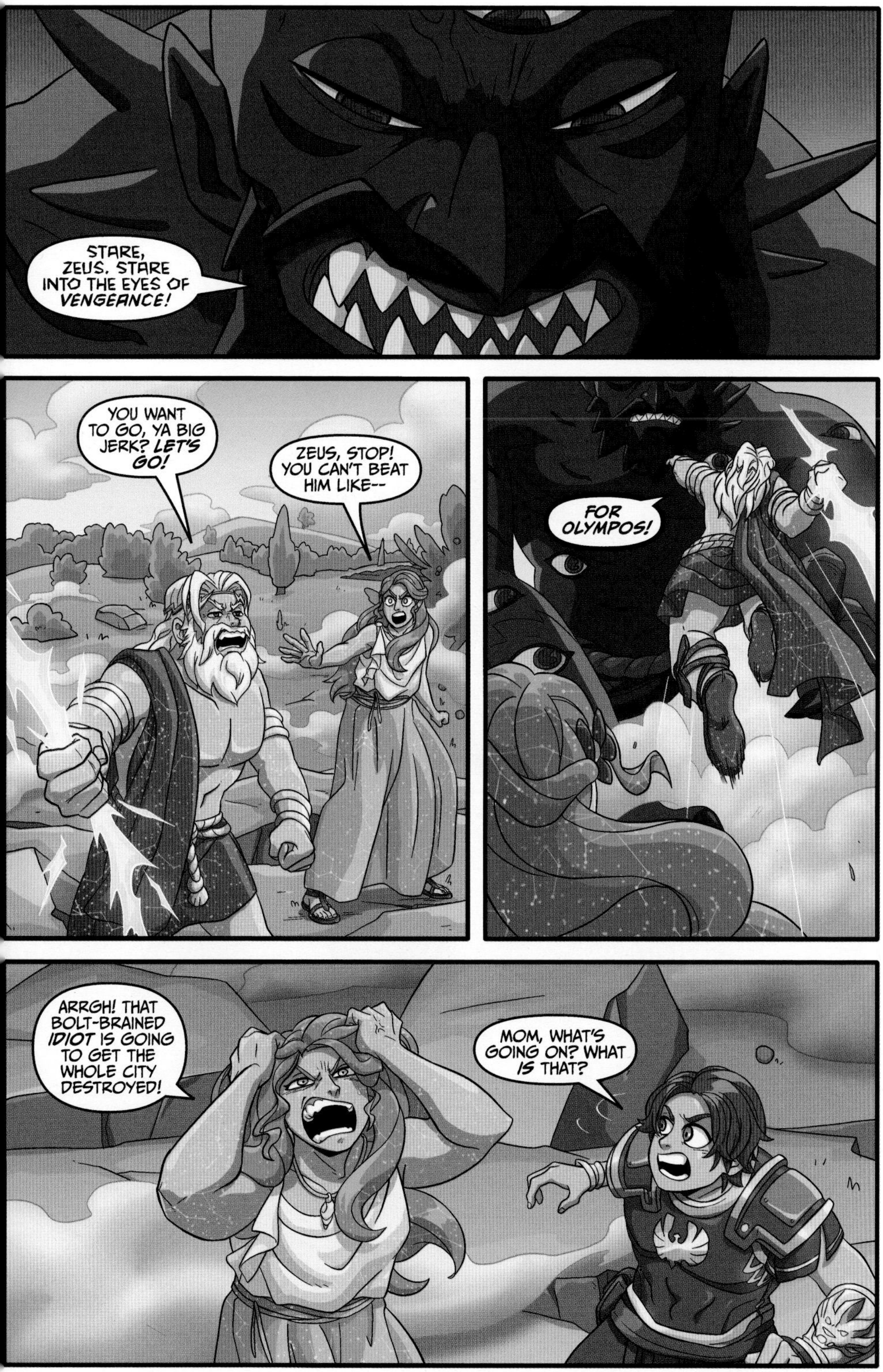
STARE, ZEUS. STARE INTO THE EYES OF *VENGEANCE!*
YOU WANT TO GO, YA BIG JERK? *LET'S GO!*
ZEUS, STOP! YOU CAN'T BEAT HIM LIKE--
FOR OLYMPOS!
ARRGH! THAT BOLT-BRAINED *IDIOT* IS GOING TO GET THE WHOLE CITY DESTROYED!
MOM, WHAT'S GOING ON? WHAT *IS* THAT?

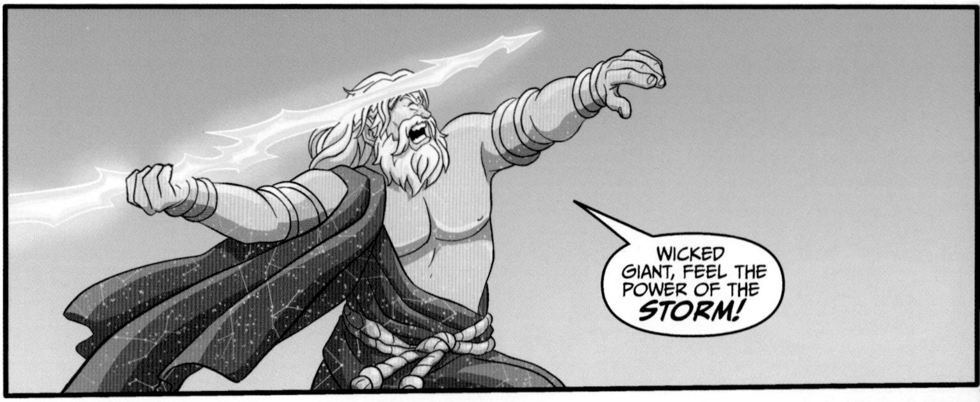
WICKED GIANT, FEEL THE POWER OF THE STORM!

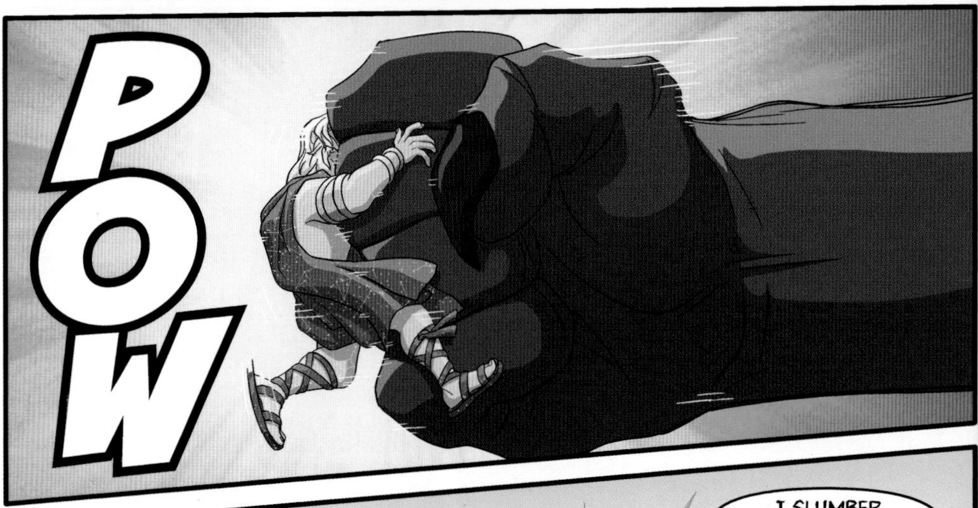
POW

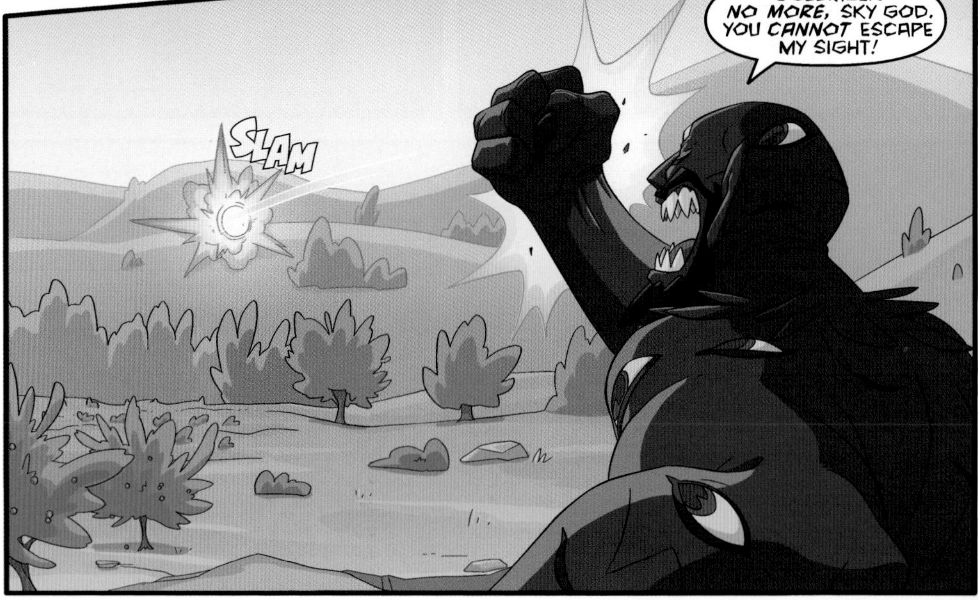
I SLUMBER NO MORE, SKY GOD. YOU CANNOT ESCAPE MY SIGHT!
SLAM

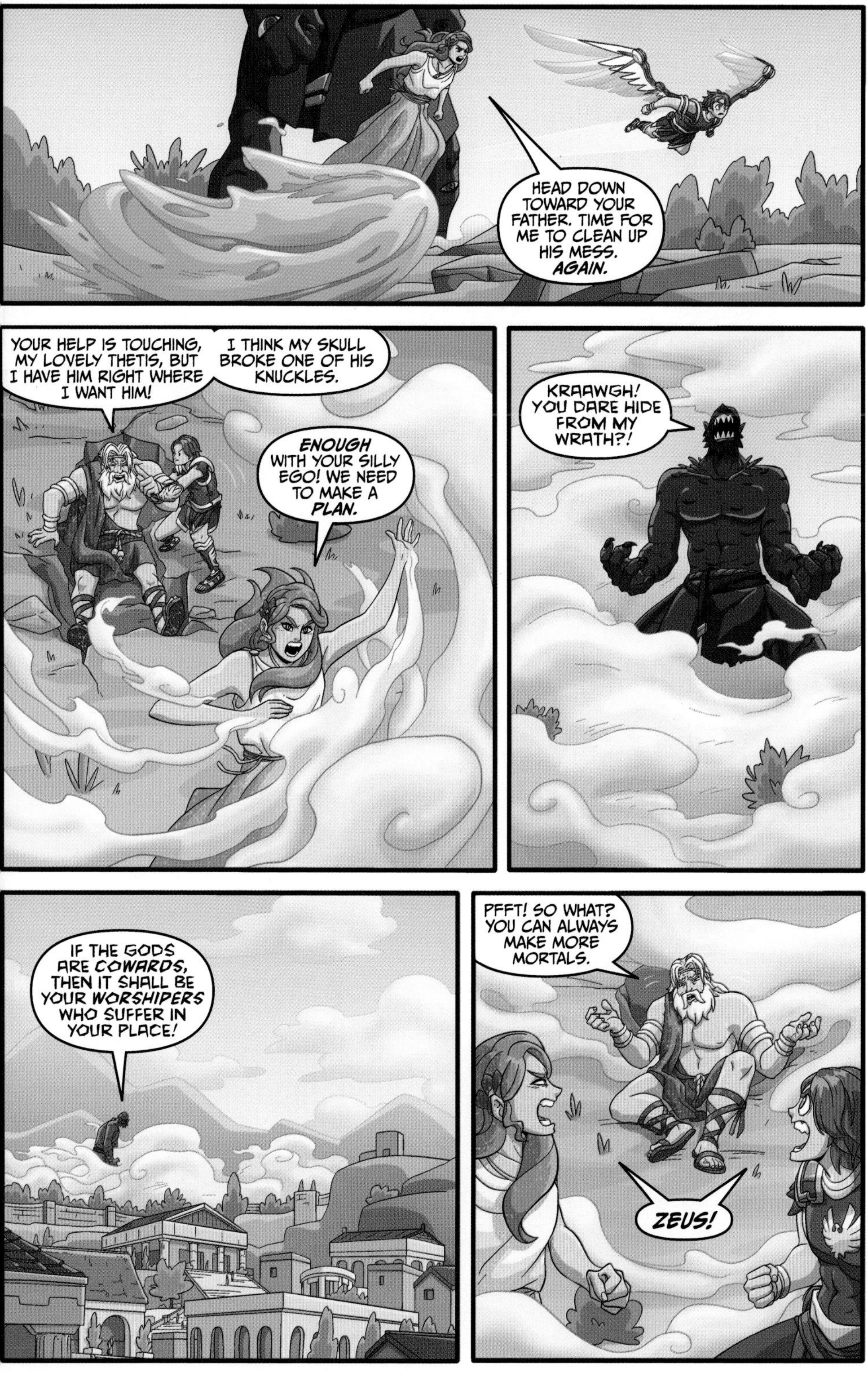
HEAD DOWN TOWARD YOUR FATHER. TIME FOR ME TO CLEAN UP HIS MESS. AGAIN.
YOUR HELP IS TOUCHING, MY LOVELY THETIS, BUT I HAVE HIM RIGHT WHERE I WANT HIM!
I THINK MY SKULL BROKE ONE OF HIS KNUCKLES.
ENOUGH WITH YOUR SILLY EGO! WE NEED TO MAKE A PLAN.
KRAAWGH! YOU DARE HIDE FROM MY WRATH?!
IF THE GODS ARE COWARDS, THEN IT SHALL BE YOUR WORSHIPERS WHO SUFFER IN YOUR PLACE!
PFFT! SO WHAT? YOU CAN ALWAYS MAKE MORE MORTALS.
ZEUS!

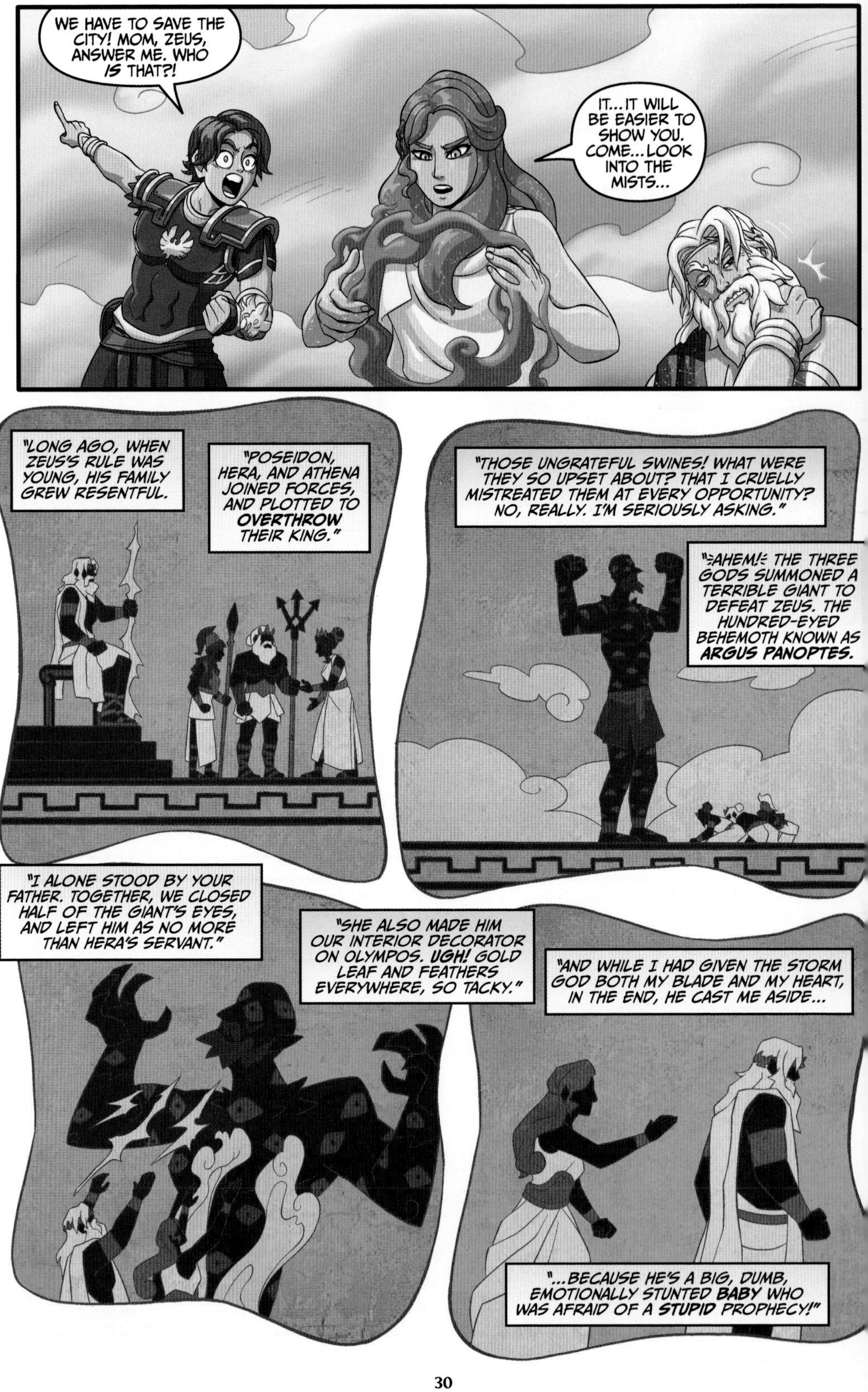
WE HAVE TO SAVE THE CITY! MOM, ZEUS, ANSWER ME. WHO *IS* THAT?!
IT... IT WILL BE EASIER TO SHOW YOU. COME... LOOK INTO THE MISTS...
"LONG AGO, WHEN ZEUS'S RULE WAS YOUNG, HIS FAMILY GREW RESENTFUL.
"POSEIDON, HERA, AND ATHENA JOINED FORCES, AND PLOTTED TO **OVERTHROW** THEIR KING."
"THOSE UNGRATEFUL SWINES! WHAT WERE THEY SO UPSET ABOUT? THAT I CRUELLY MISTREATED THEM AT EVERY OPPORTUNITY? NO, REALLY. I'M SERIOUSLY ASKING."
"AHEM! THE THREE GODS SUMMONED A TERRIBLE GIANT TO DEFEAT ZEUS. THE HUNDRED-EYED BEHEMOTH KNOWN AS **ARGUS PANOPTES.**
"I ALONE STOOD BY YOUR FATHER. TOGETHER, WE CLOSED HALF OF THE GIANT'S EYES, AND LEFT HIM AS NO MORE THAN HERA'S SERVANT."
"SHE ALSO MADE HIM OUR INTERIOR DECORATOR ON OLYMPOS. **UGH!** GOLD LEAF AND FEATHERS EVERYWHERE, SO TACKY."
"AND WHILE I HAD GIVEN THE STORM GOD BOTH MY BLADE AND MY HEART, IN THE END, HE CAST ME ASIDE...
"...BECAUSE HE'S A BIG, DUMB, EMOTIONALLY STUNTED **BABY** WHO WAS AFRAID OF A **STUPID** PROPHECY!"

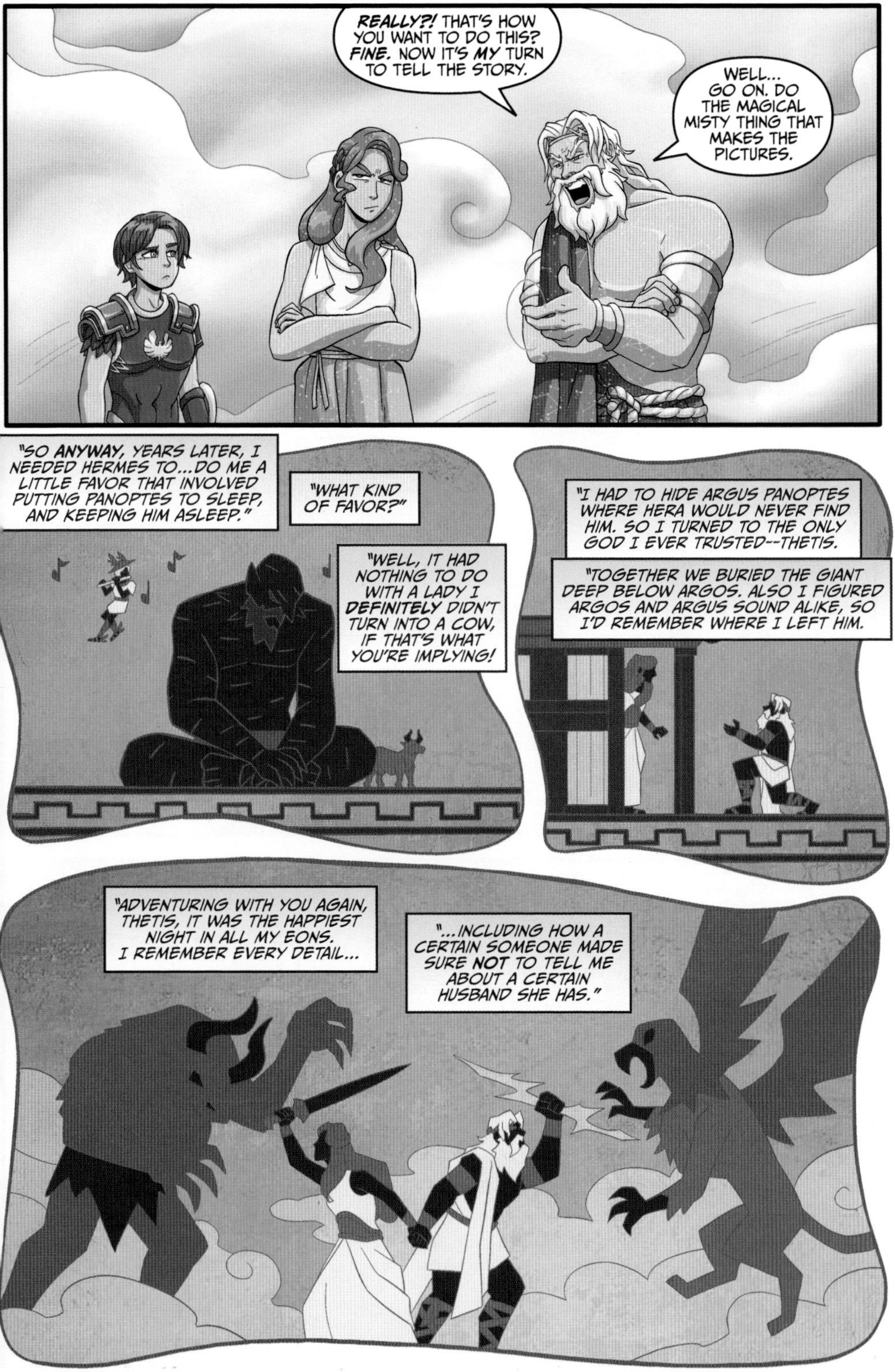
REALLY?! THAT'S HOW YOU WANT TO DO THIS? FINE. NOW IT'S MY TURN TO TELL THE STORY.
WELL... GO ON. DO THE MAGICAL MISTY THING THAT MAKES THE PICTURES.
"SO ANYWAY, YEARS LATER, I NEEDED HERMES TO...DO ME A LITTLE FAVOR THAT INVOLVED PUTTING PANOPTES TO SLEEP, AND KEEPING HIM ASLEEP."
"WHAT KIND OF FAVOR?"
"WELL, IT HAD NOTHING TO DO WITH A LADY I DEFINITELY DIDN'T TURN INTO A COW, IF THAT'S WHAT YOU'RE IMPLYING!
"I HAD TO HIDE ARGUS PANOPTES WHERE HERA WOULD NEVER FIND HIM. SO I TURNED TO THE ONLY GOD I EVER TRUSTED--THETIS.
"TOGETHER WE BURIED THE GIANT DEEP BELOW ARGOS. ALSO I FIGURED ARGOS AND ARGUS SOUND ALIKE, SO I'D REMEMBER WHERE I LEFT HIM.
"ADVENTURING WITH YOU AGAIN, THETIS, IT WAS THE HAPPIEST NIGHT IN ALL MY EONS. I REMEMBER EVERY DETAIL...
"...INCLUDING HOW A CERTAIN SOMEONE MADE SURE NOT TO TELL ME ABOUT A CERTAIN HUSBAND SHE HAS."

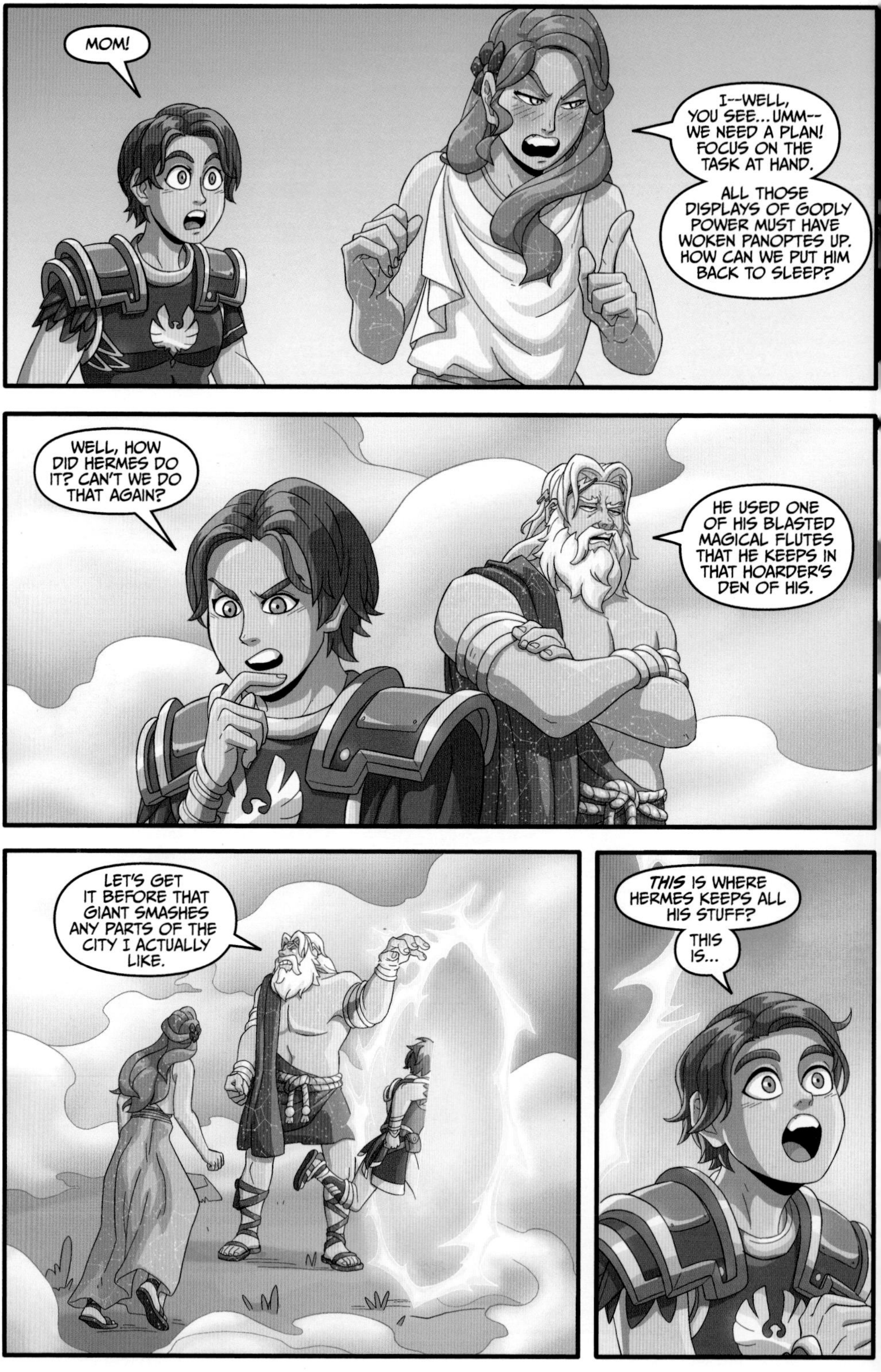
MOM!
I--WELL, YOU SEE...UMM-- WE NEED A PLAN! FOCUS ON THE TASK AT HAND.
ALL THOSE DISPLAYS OF GODLY POWER MUST HAVE WOKEN PANOPTES UP. HOW CAN WE PUT HIM BACK TO SLEEP?
WELL, HOW DID HERMES DO IT? CAN'T WE DO THAT AGAIN?
HE USED ONE OF HIS BLASTED MAGICAL FLUTES THAT HE KEEPS IN THAT HOARDER'S DEN OF HIS.
LET'S GET IT BEFORE THAT GIANT SMASHES ANY PARTS OF THE CITY I ACTUALLY LIKE.
THIS IS WHERE HERMES KEEPS ALL HIS STUFF?
THIS IS...

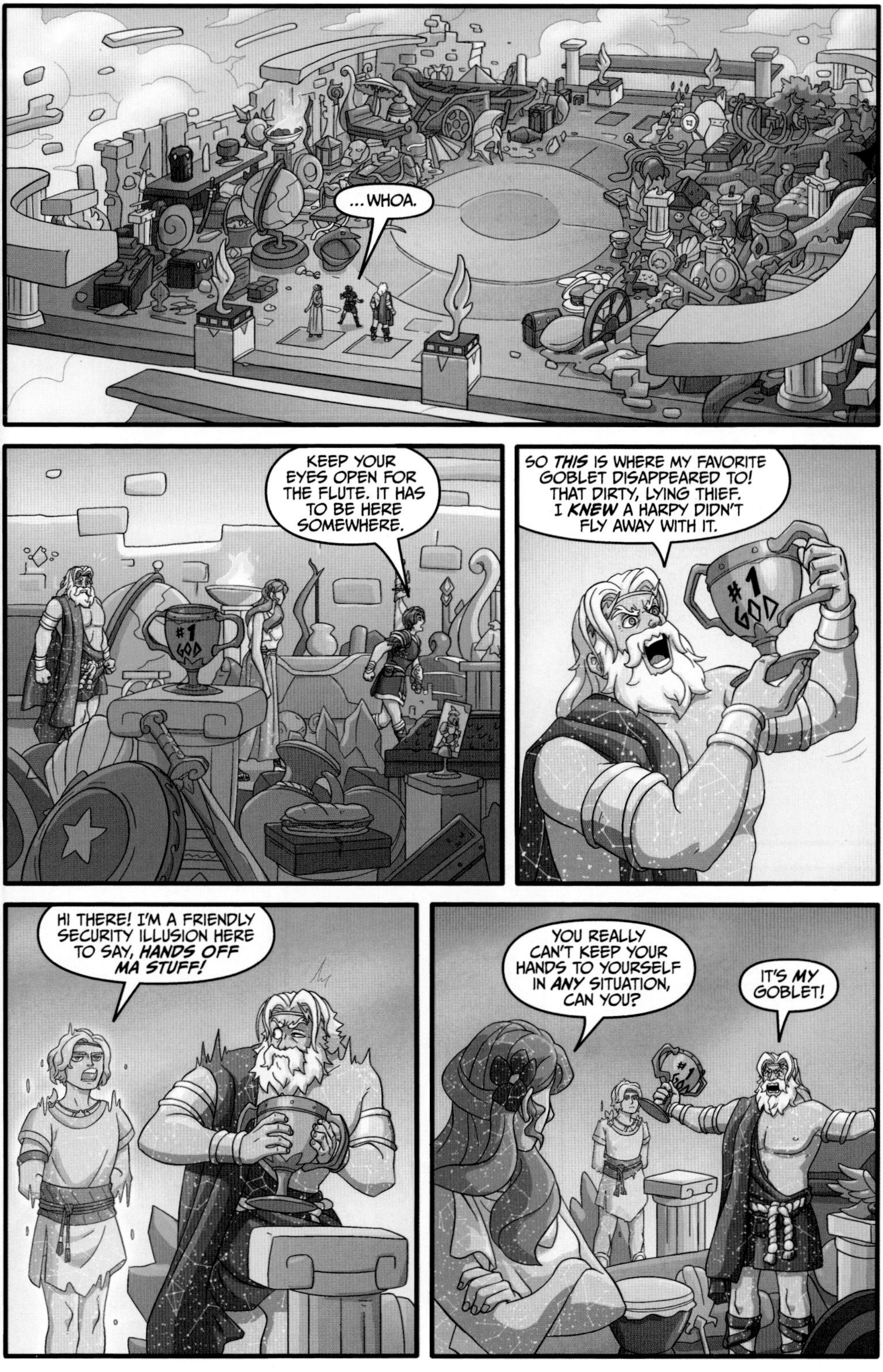
...WHOA.
KEEP YOUR EYES OPEN FOR THE FLUTE. IT HAS TO BE HERE SOMEWHERE.
#1 GOD
SO THIS IS WHERE MY FAVORITE GOBLET DISAPPEARED TO! THAT DIRTY, LYING THIEF. I KNEW A HARPY DIDN'T FLY AWAY WITH IT.
#1 GOD
HI THERE! I'M A FRIENDLY SECURITY ILLUSION HERE TO SAY, HANDS OFF MA STUFF!
YOU REALLY CAN'T KEEP YOUR HANDS TO YOURSELF IN ANY SITUATION, CAN YOU?
IT'S MY GOBLET!

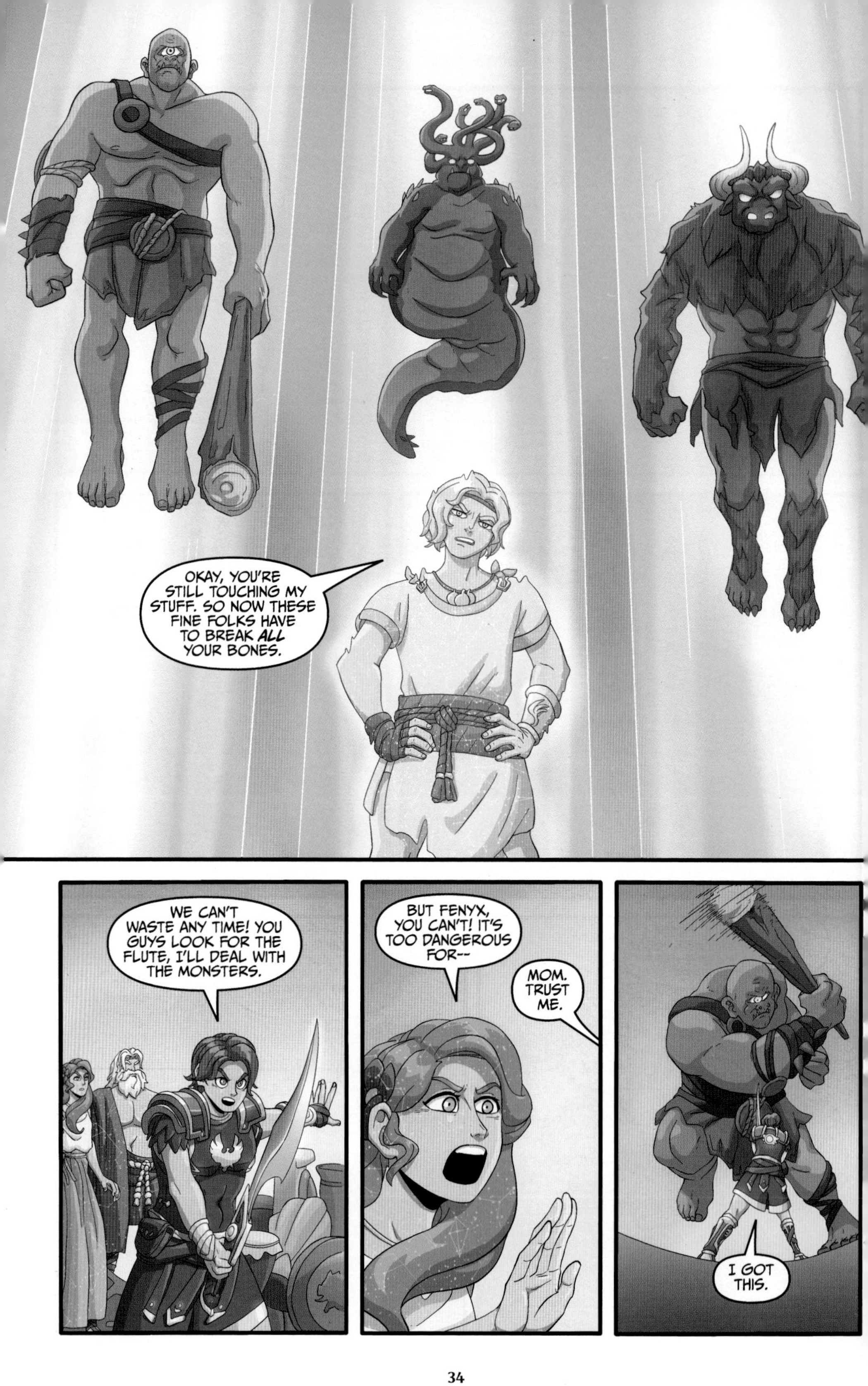
OKAY, YOU'RE STILL TOUCHING MY STUFF. SO NOW THESE FINE FOLKS HAVE TO BREAK ALL YOUR BONES.
WE CAN'T WASTE ANY TIME! YOU GUYS LOOK FOR THE FLUTE, I'LL DEAL WITH THE MONSTERS.
BUT FENYX, YOU CAN'T! IT'S TOO DANGEROUS FOR--
MOM. TRUST ME.
I GOT THIS.

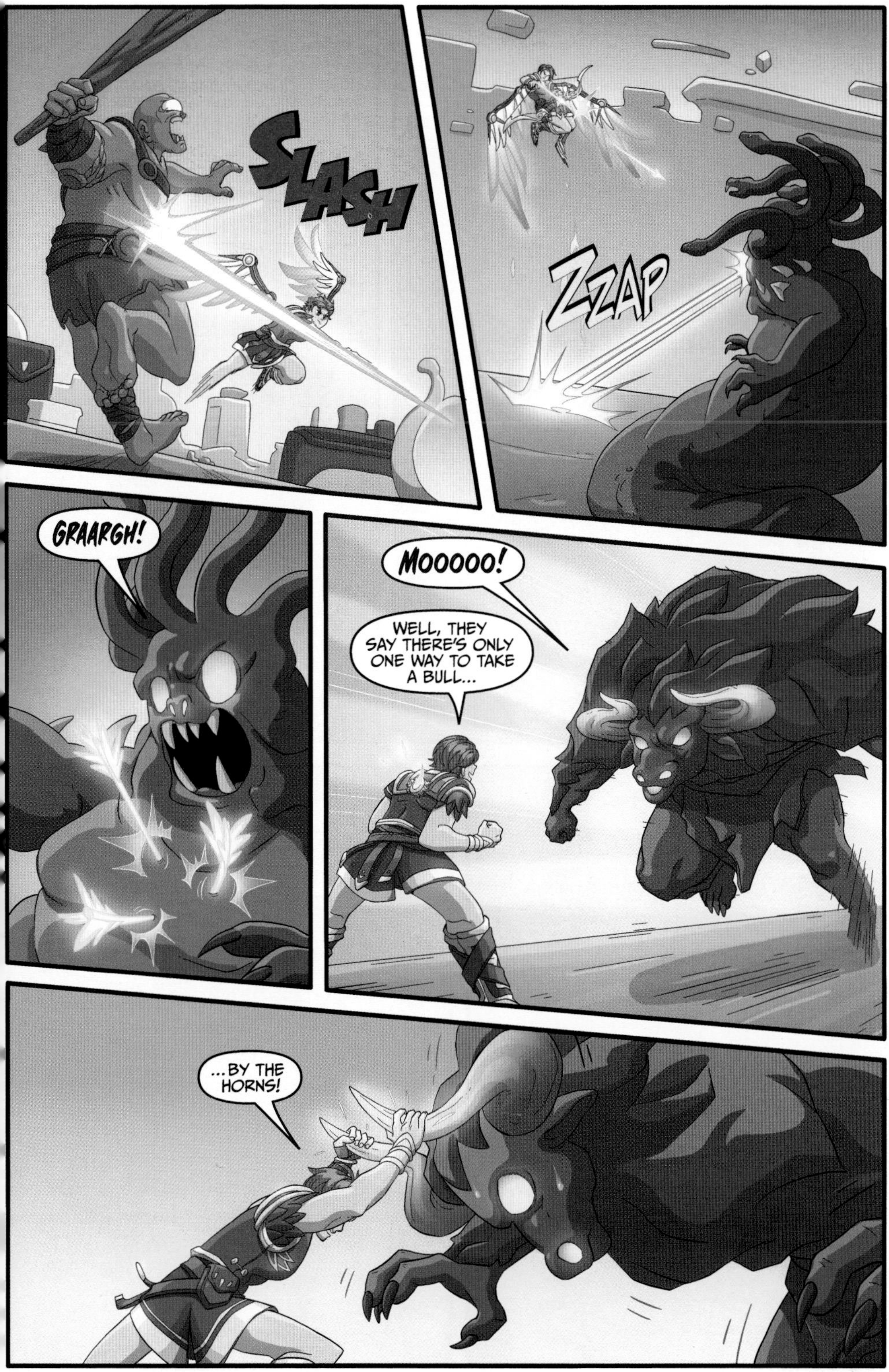
SLASH
ZZAP
GRAARGH!
MOOOOO!
WELL, THEY SAY THERE'S ONLY ONE WAY TO TAKE A BULL...
...BY THE HORNS!

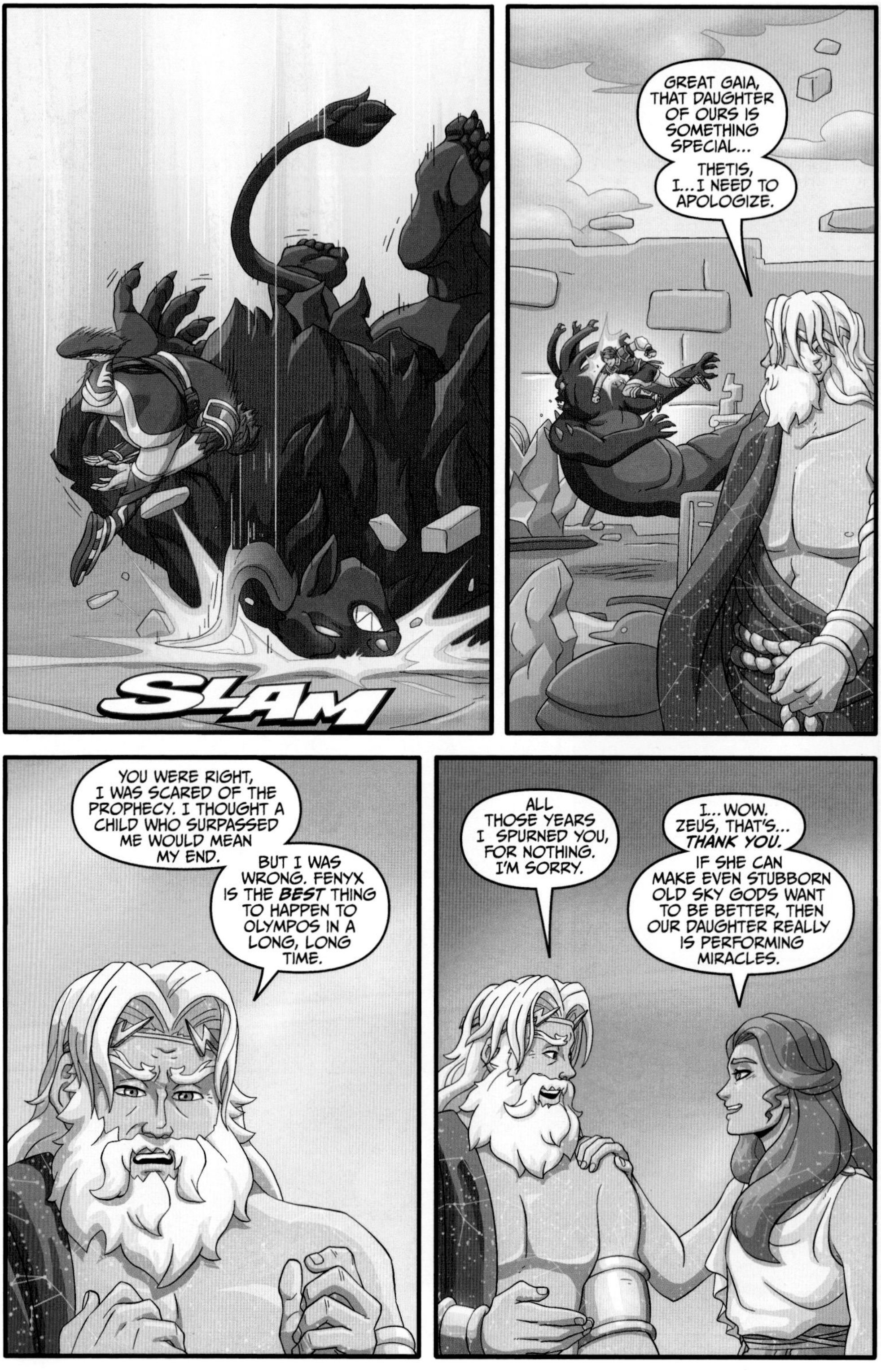
SLAM
GREAT GAIA, THAT DAUGHTER OF OURS IS SOMETHING SPECIAL...
THETIS, I...I NEED TO APOLOGIZE.
YOU WERE RIGHT, I WAS SCARED OF THE PROPHECY. I THOUGHT A CHILD WHO SURPASSED ME WOULD MEAN MY END.
BUT I WAS WRONG. FENYX IS THE **BEST** THING TO HAPPEN TO OLYMPOS IN A LONG, LONG TIME.
ALL THOSE YEARS I SPURNED YOU, FOR NOTHING. I'M SORRY.
I...WOW. ZEUS, THAT'S... ***THANK YOU.***
IF SHE CAN MAKE EVEN STUBBORN OLD SKY GODS WANT TO BE BETTER, THEN OUR DAUGHTER REALLY IS PERFORMING MIRACLES.

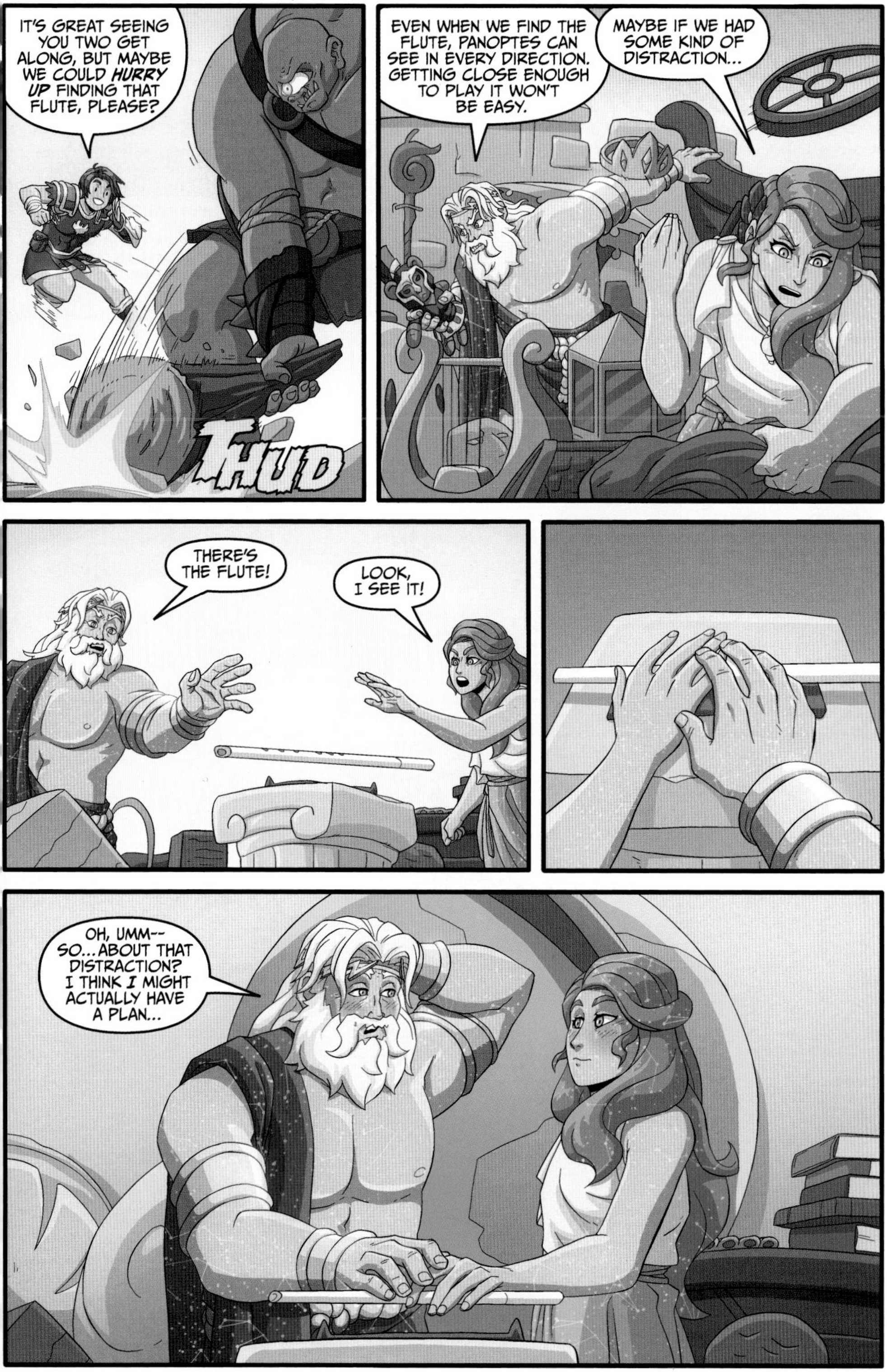
IT'S GREAT SEEING YOU TWO GET ALONG, BUT MAYBE WE COULD HURRY UP FINDING THAT FLUTE, PLEASE?
THUD
EVEN WHEN WE FIND THE FLUTE, PANOPTES CAN SEE IN EVERY DIRECTION. GETTING CLOSE ENOUGH TO PLAY IT WON'T BE EASY.
MAYBE IF WE HAD SOME KIND OF DISTRACTION...
THERE'S THE FLUTE!
LOOK, I SEE IT!
OH, UMM-- SO...ABOUT THAT DISTRACTION? I THINK I MIGHT ACTUALLY HAVE A PLAN...

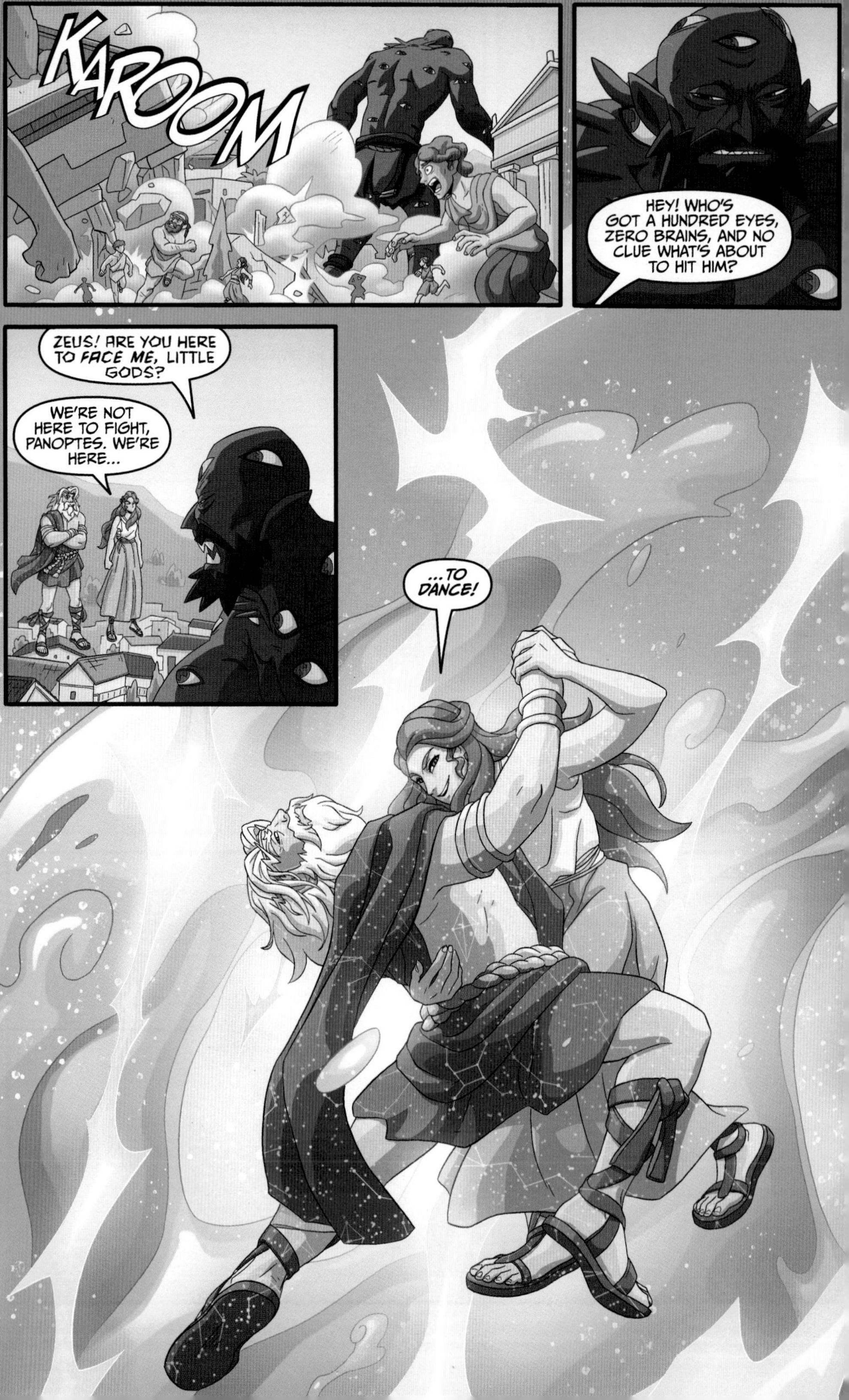
KAROOM
HEY! WHO'S GOT A HUNDRED EYES, ZERO BRAINS, AND NO CLUE WHAT'S ABOUT TO HIT HIM?
ZEUS! ARE YOU HERE TO FACE ME, LITTLE GODS?
WE'RE NOT HERE TO FIGHT, PANOPTES. WE'RE HERE...
...TO DANCE!

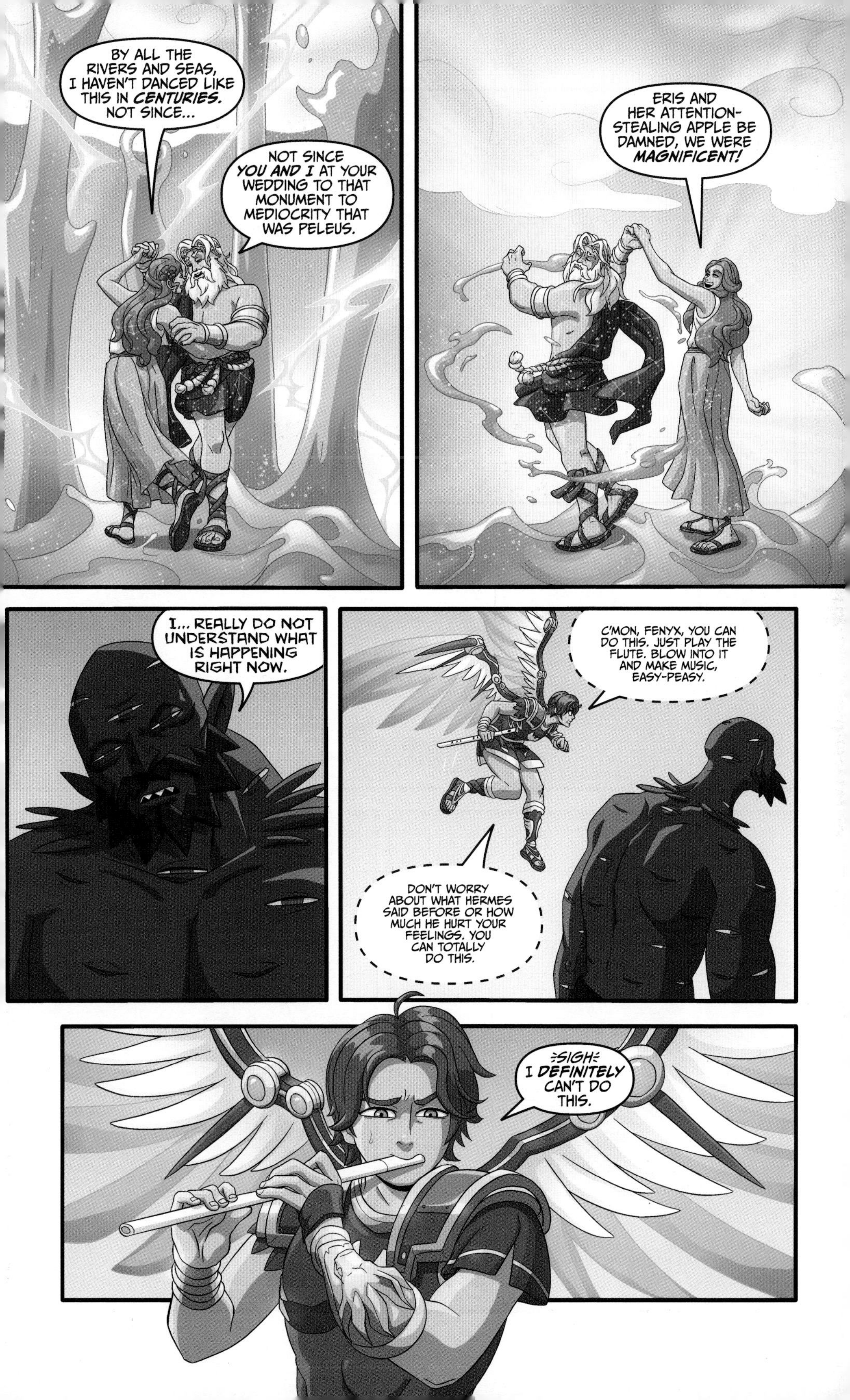
BY ALL THE RIVERS AND SEAS, I HAVEN'T DANCED LIKE THIS IN *CENTURIES.* NOT SINCE...
NOT SINCE *YOU AND I* AT YOUR WEDDING TO THAT MONUMENT TO MEDIOCRITY THAT WAS PELEUS.
ERIS AND HER ATTENTION-STEALING APPLE BE DAMNED, WE WERE *MAGNIFICENT!*
I... REALLY DO NOT UNDERSTAND WHAT IS HAPPENING RIGHT NOW.
C'MON, FENYX, YOU CAN DO THIS. JUST PLAY THE FLUTE. BLOW INTO IT AND MAKE MUSIC, EASY-PEASY.
DON'T WORRY ABOUT WHAT HERMES SAID BEFORE OR HOW MUCH HE HURT YOUR FEELINGS. YOU CAN TOTALLY DO THIS.
SIGH
I *DEFINITELY* CAN'T DO THIS.

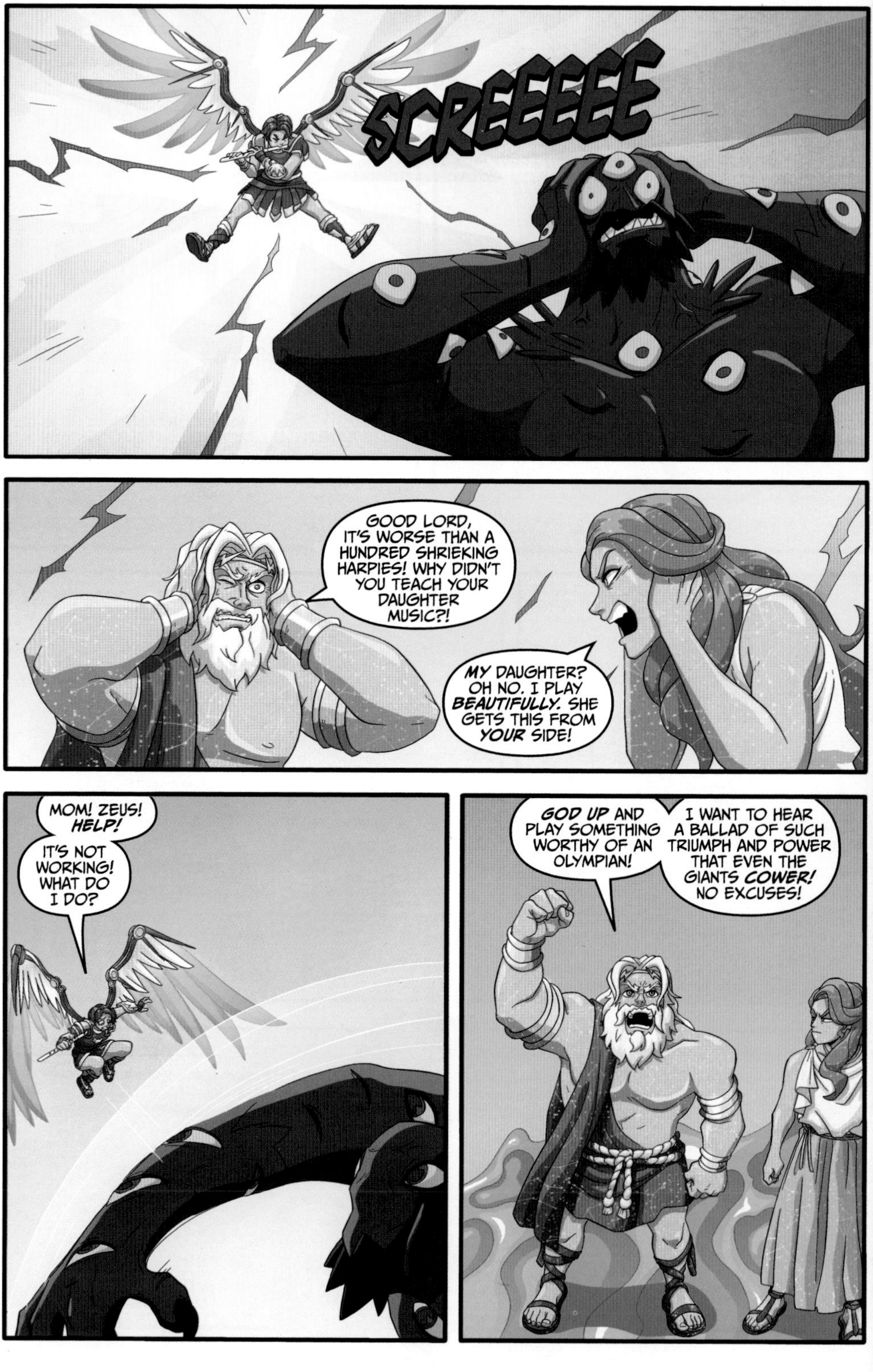
SCREEEEEE
GOOD LORD, IT'S WORSE THAN A HUNDRED SHRIEKING HARPIES! WHY DIDN'T YOU TEACH YOUR DAUGHTER MUSIC?!
MY DAUGHTER? OH NO. I PLAY *BEAUTIFULLY.* SHE GETS THIS FROM *YOUR* SIDE!
MOM! ZEUS! *HELP!*
IT'S NOT WORKING! WHAT DO I DO?
GOD UP AND PLAY SOMETHING WORTHY OF AN OLYMPIAN!
I WANT TO HEAR A BALLAD OF SUCH TRIUMPH AND POWER THAT EVEN THE GIANTS *COWER!* NO EXCUSES!

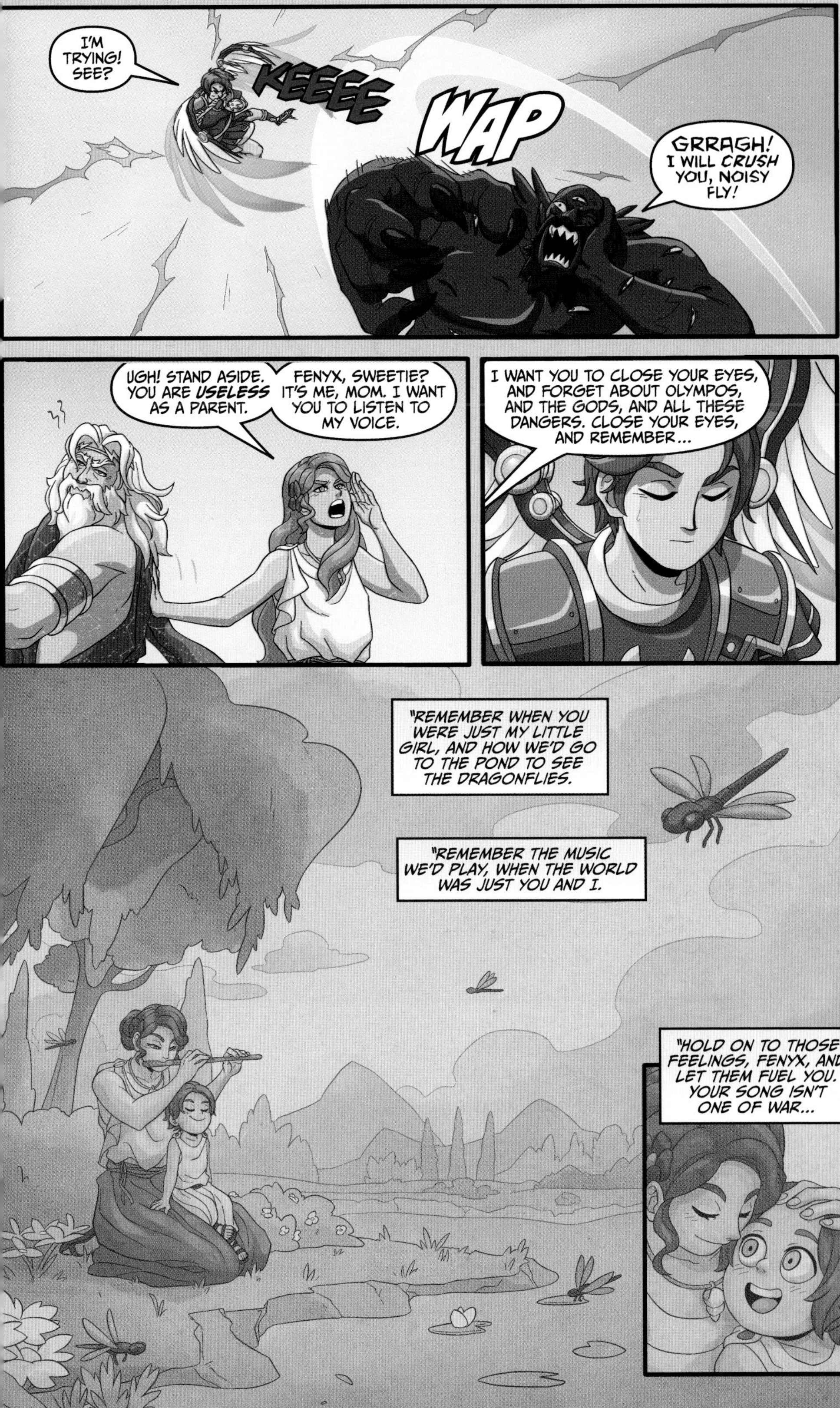
I'M TRYING! SEE?
KEEEEE
WAP
GRRAGH! I WILL *CRUSH* YOU, NOISY FLY!
UGH! STAND ASIDE. YOU ARE ***USELESS*** AS A PARENT.
FENYX, SWEETIE? IT'S ME, MOM. I WANT YOU TO LISTEN TO MY VOICE.
I WANT YOU TO CLOSE YOUR EYES, AND FORGET ABOUT OLYMPOS, AND THE GODS, AND ALL THESE DANGERS. CLOSE YOUR EYES, AND REMEMBER...
"REMEMBER WHEN YOU WERE JUST MY LITTLE GIRL, AND HOW WE'D GO TO THE POND TO SEE THE DRAGONFLIES.
"REMEMBER THE MUSIC WE'D PLAY, WHEN THE WORLD WAS JUST YOU AND I.
"HOLD ON TO THOSE FEELINGS, FENYX, AND LET THEM FUEL YOU. YOUR SONG ISN'T ONE OF WAR...

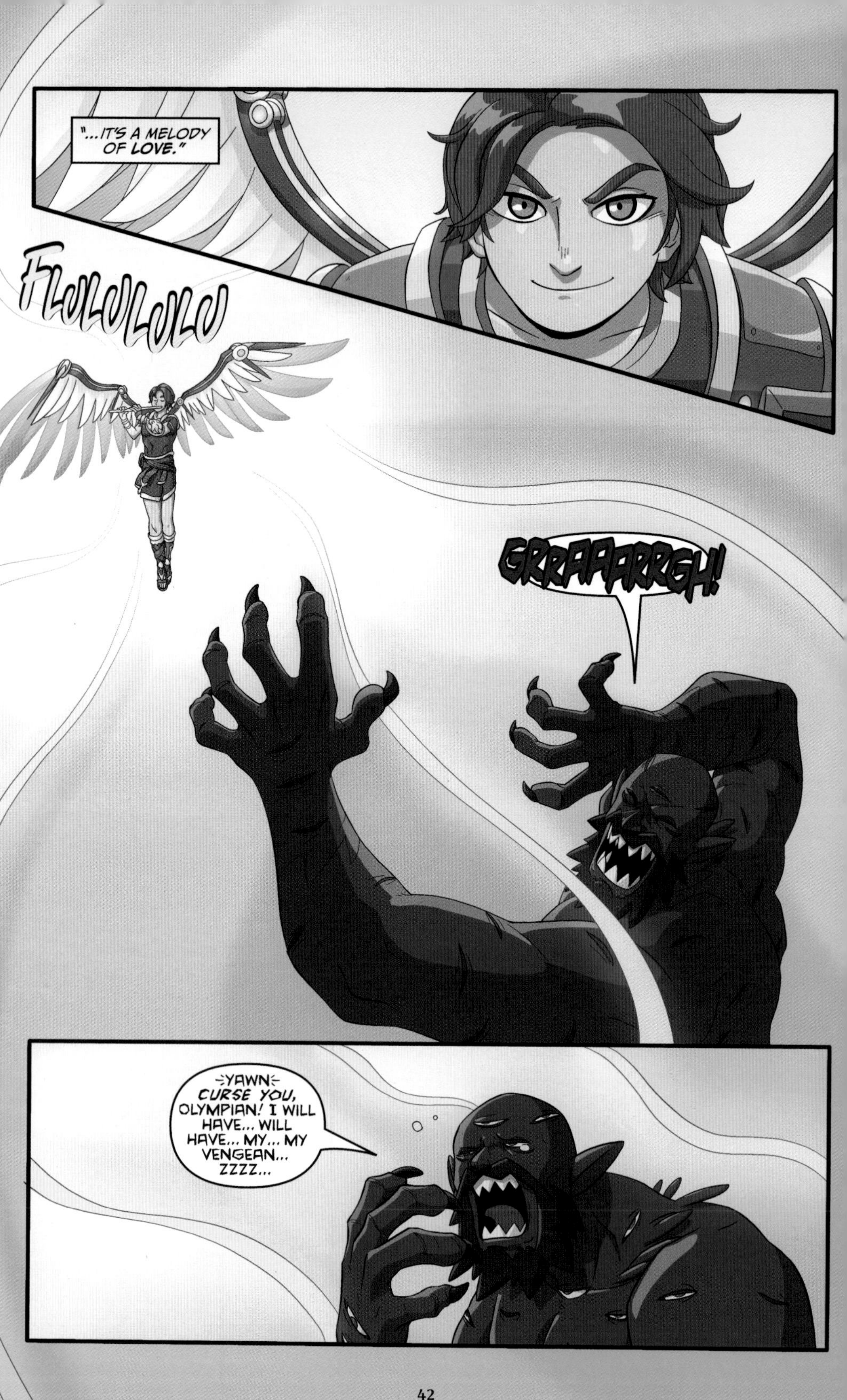
"...IT'S A MELODY OF LOVE."
FLULULULU
GRRAAARRGH!
=YAWN= CURSE YOU, OLYMPIAN! I WILL HAVE... WILL HAVE... MY... MY VENGEAN... ZZZZ...

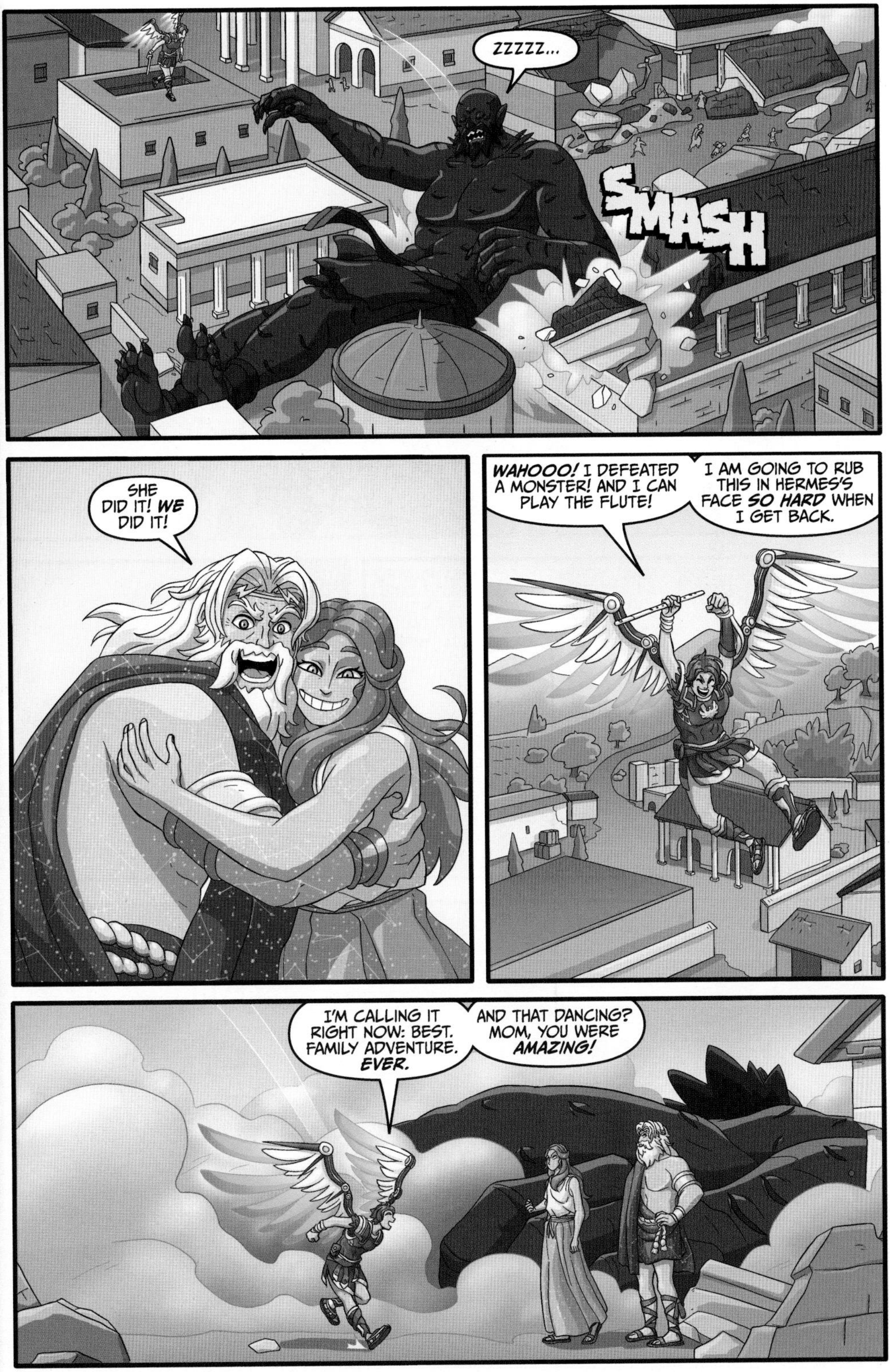
ZZZZZ...
SMASH
SHE DID IT! WE DID IT!
WAHOOO! I DEFEATED A MONSTER! AND I CAN PLAY THE FLUTE!
I AM GOING TO RUB THIS IN HERMES'S FACE SO HARD WHEN I GET BACK.
I'M CALLING IT RIGHT NOW: BEST. FAMILY ADVENTURE. EVER.
AND THAT DANCING? MOM, YOU WERE AMAZING!

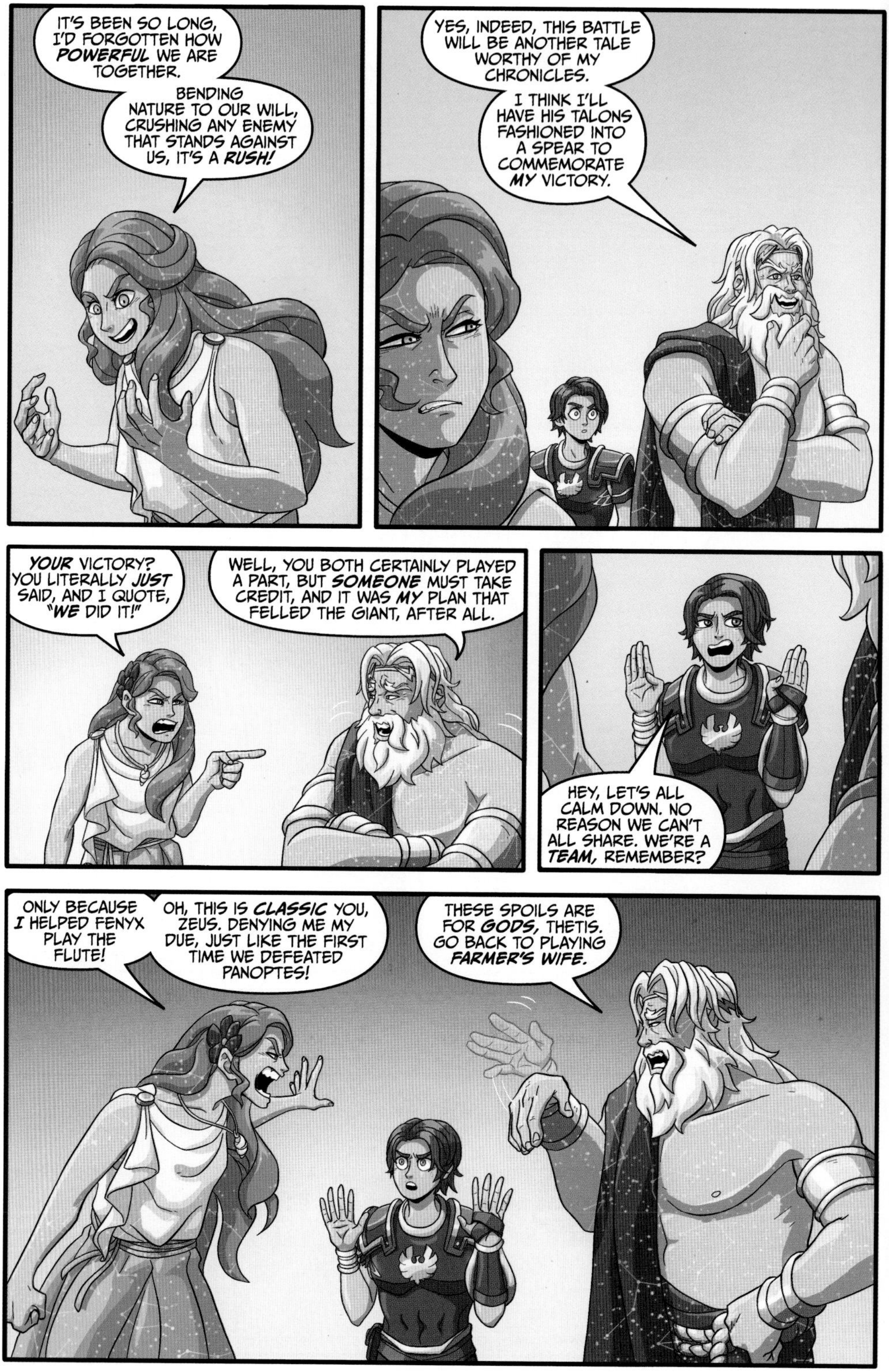
IT'S BEEN SO LONG, I'D FORGOTTEN HOW POWERFUL WE ARE TOGETHER.
BENDING NATURE TO OUR WILL, CRUSHING ANY ENEMY THAT STANDS AGAINST US, IT'S A RUSH!
YES, INDEED, THIS BATTLE WILL BE ANOTHER TALE WORTHY OF MY CHRONICLES.
I THINK I'LL HAVE HIS TALONS FASHIONED INTO A SPEAR TO COMMEMORATE MY VICTORY.
YOUR VICTORY? YOU LITERALLY JUST SAID, AND I QUOTE, "WE DID IT!"
WELL, YOU BOTH CERTAINLY PLAYED A PART, BUT SOMEONE MUST TAKE CREDIT, AND IT WAS MY PLAN THAT FELLED THE GIANT, AFTER ALL.
HEY, LET'S ALL CALM DOWN. NO REASON WE CAN'T ALL SHARE. WE'RE A TEAM, REMEMBER?
ONLY BECAUSE I HELPED FENYX PLAY THE FLUTE!
OH, THIS IS CLASSIC YOU, ZEUS. DENYING ME MY DUE, JUST LIKE THE FIRST TIME WE DEFEATED PANOPTES!
THESE SPOILS ARE FOR GODS, THETIS. GO BACK TO PLAYING FARMER'S WIFE.

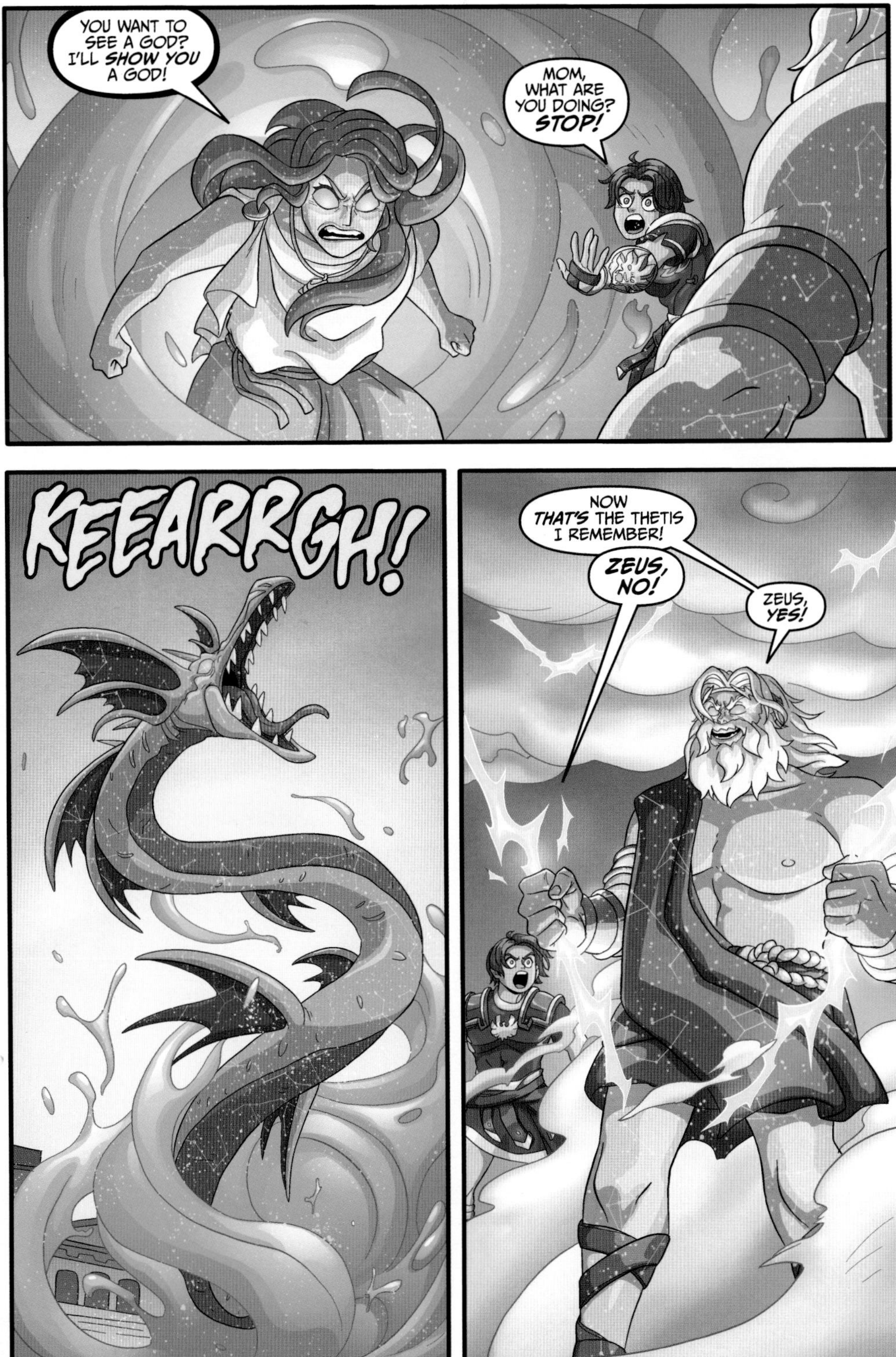
YOU WANT TO SEE A GOD? I'LL SHOW YOU A GOD!
MOM, WHAT ARE YOU DOING? STOP!
KEEARRGH!
NOW THAT'S THE THETIS I REMEMBER!
ZEUS, NO!
ZEUS, YES!

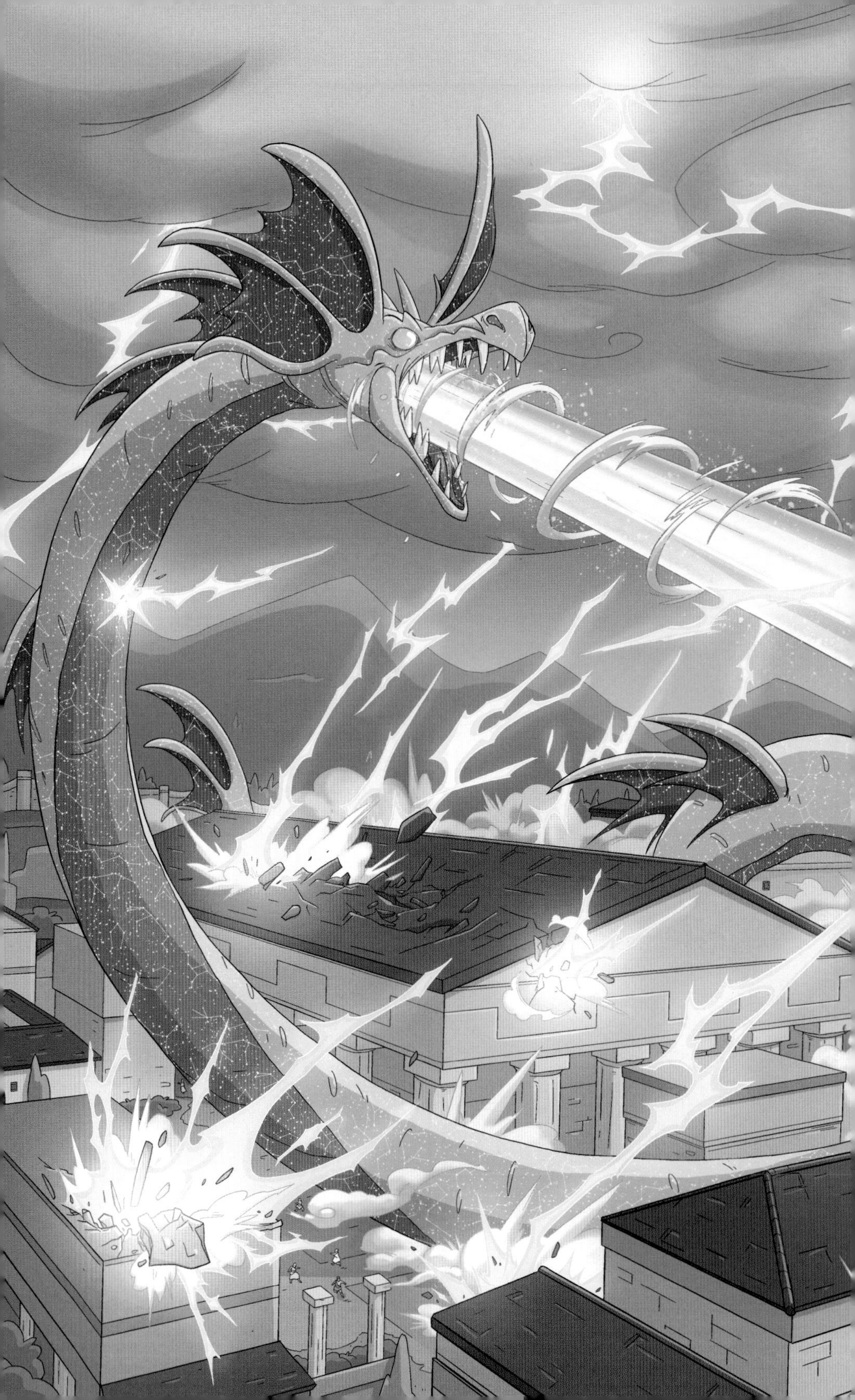

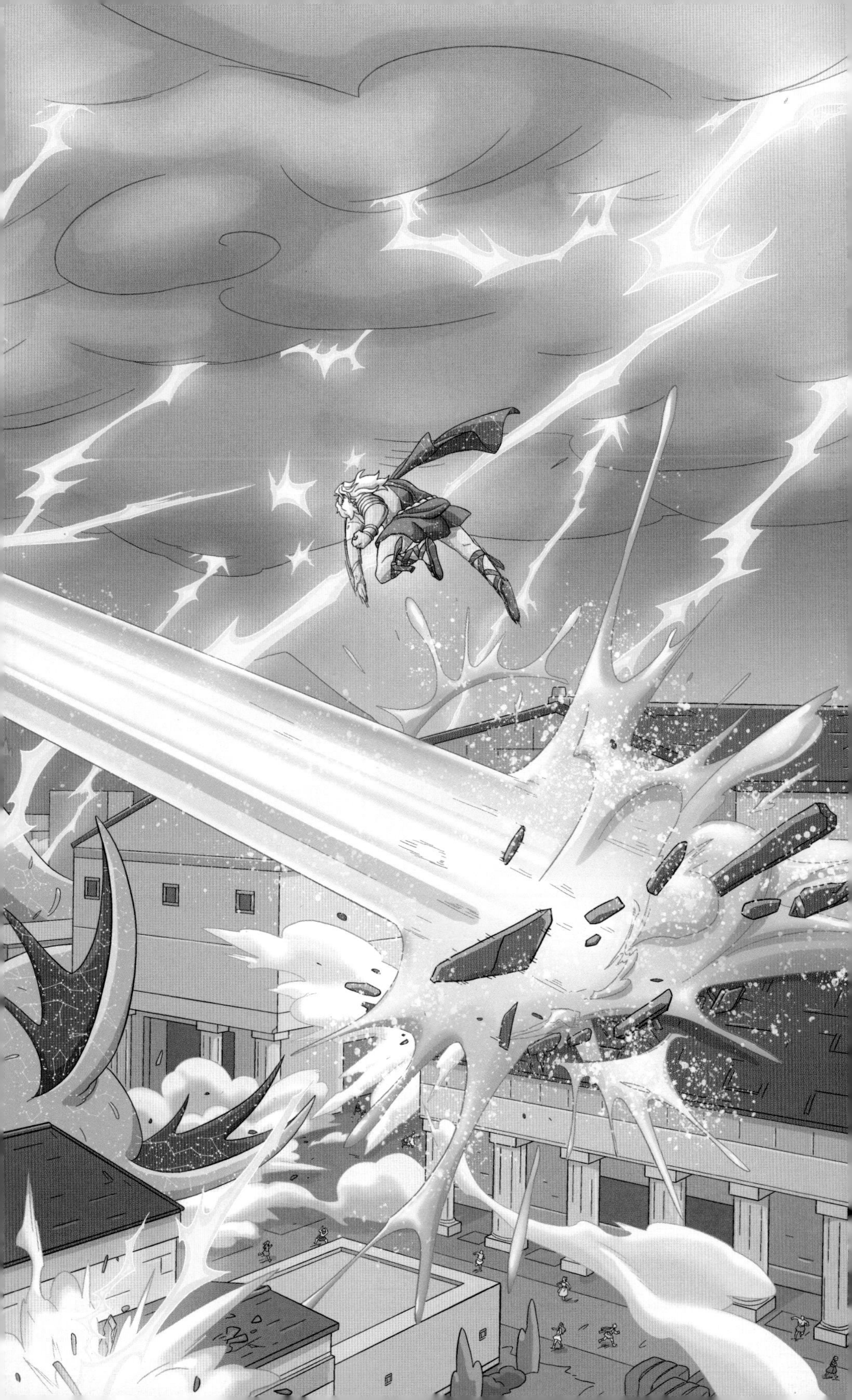

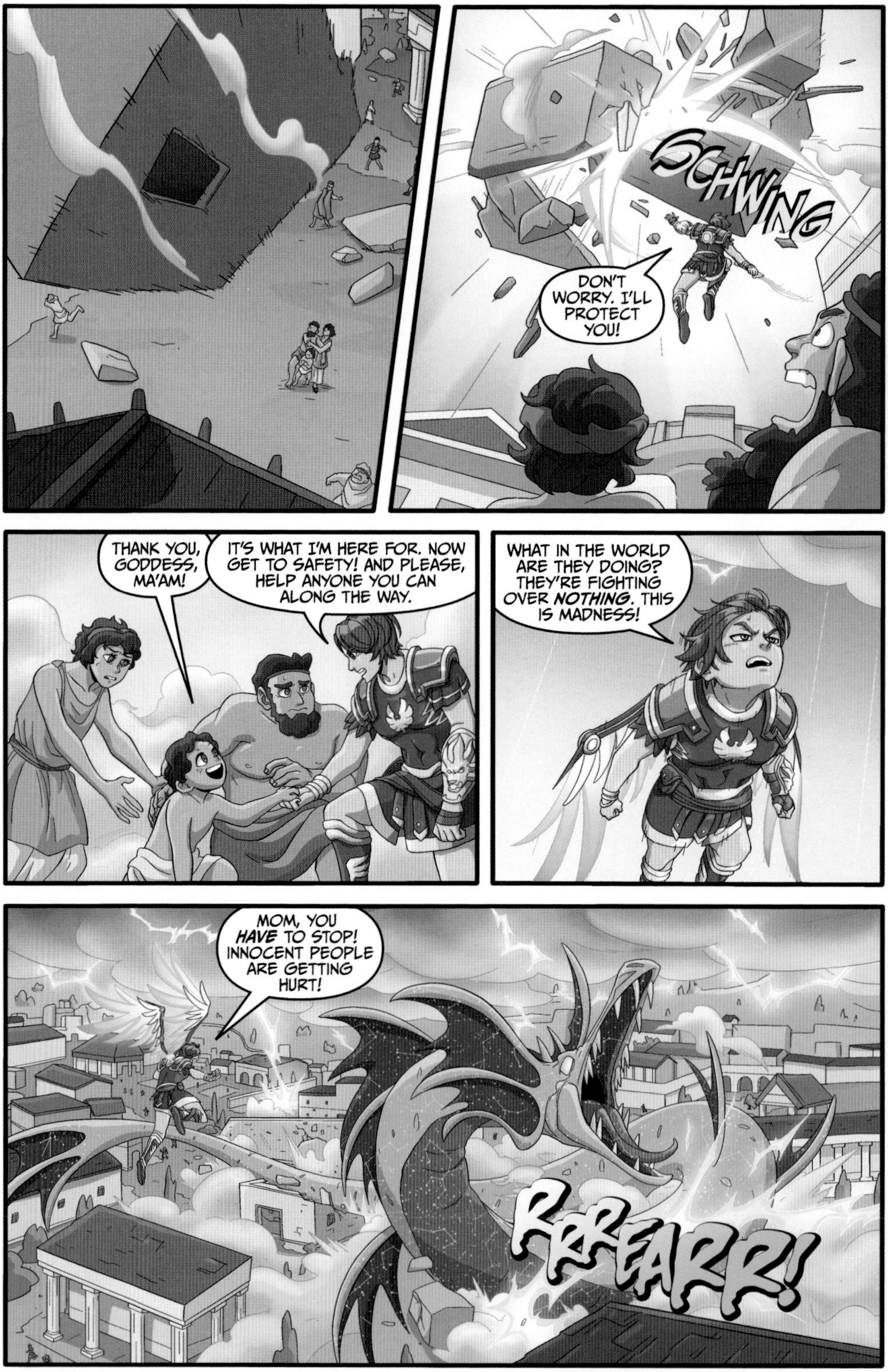
SCHWING
DON'T WORRY. I'LL PROTECT YOU!
THANK YOU, GODDESS, MA'AM!
IT'S WHAT I'M HERE FOR. NOW GET TO SAFETY! AND PLEASE, HELP ANYONE YOU CAN ALONG THE WAY.
WHAT IN THE WORLD ARE THEY DOING? THEY'RE FIGHTING OVER NOTHING. THIS IS MADNESS!
MOM, YOU HAVE TO STOP! INNOCENT PEOPLE ARE GETTING HURT!
RRREARR!

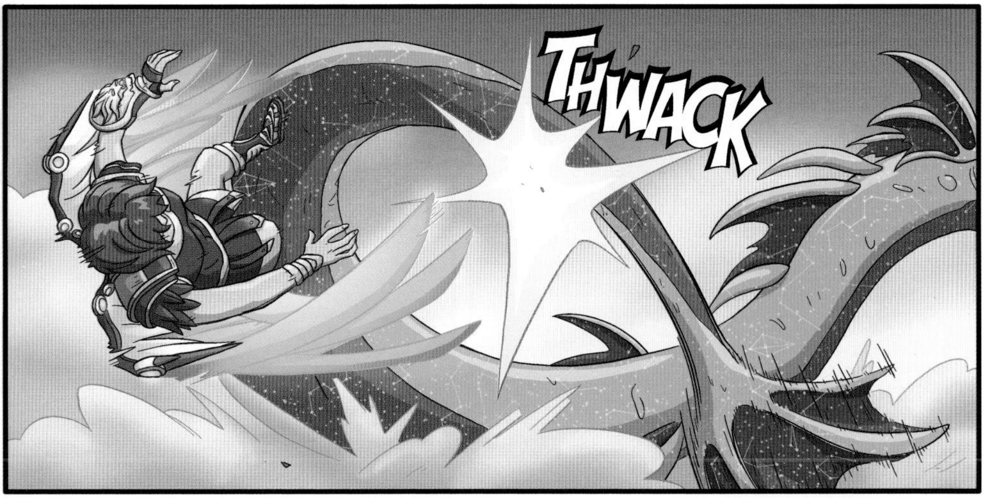
THWACK

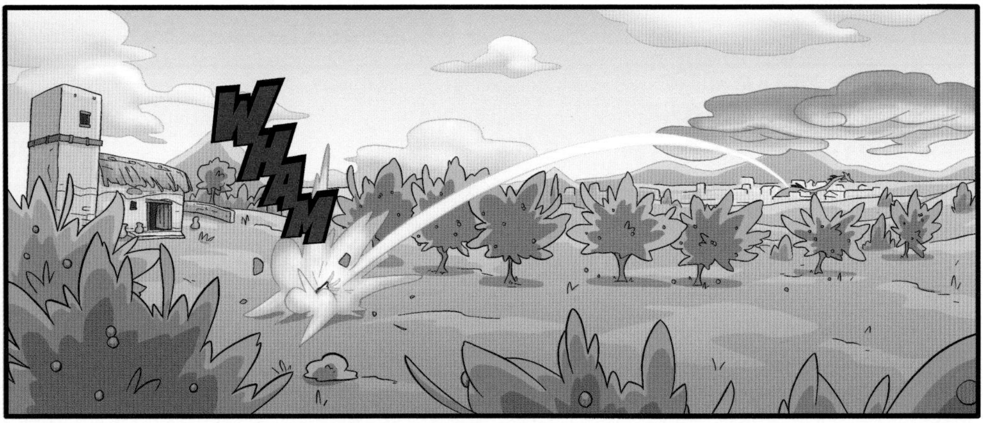
WHAM

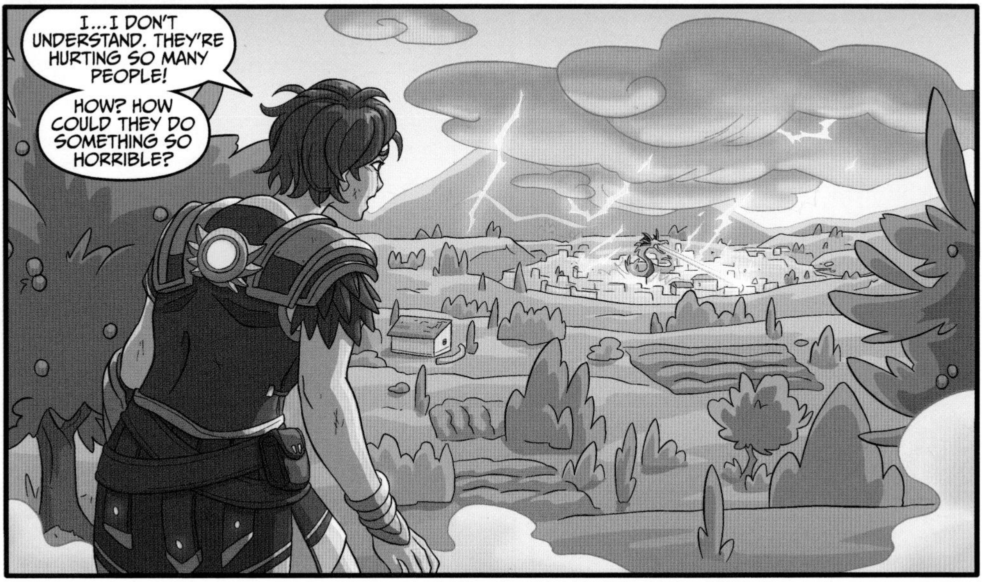
I...I DON'T UNDERSTAND. THEY'RE HURTING SO MANY PEOPLE!
HOW? HOW COULD THEY DO SOMETHING SO HORRIBLE?

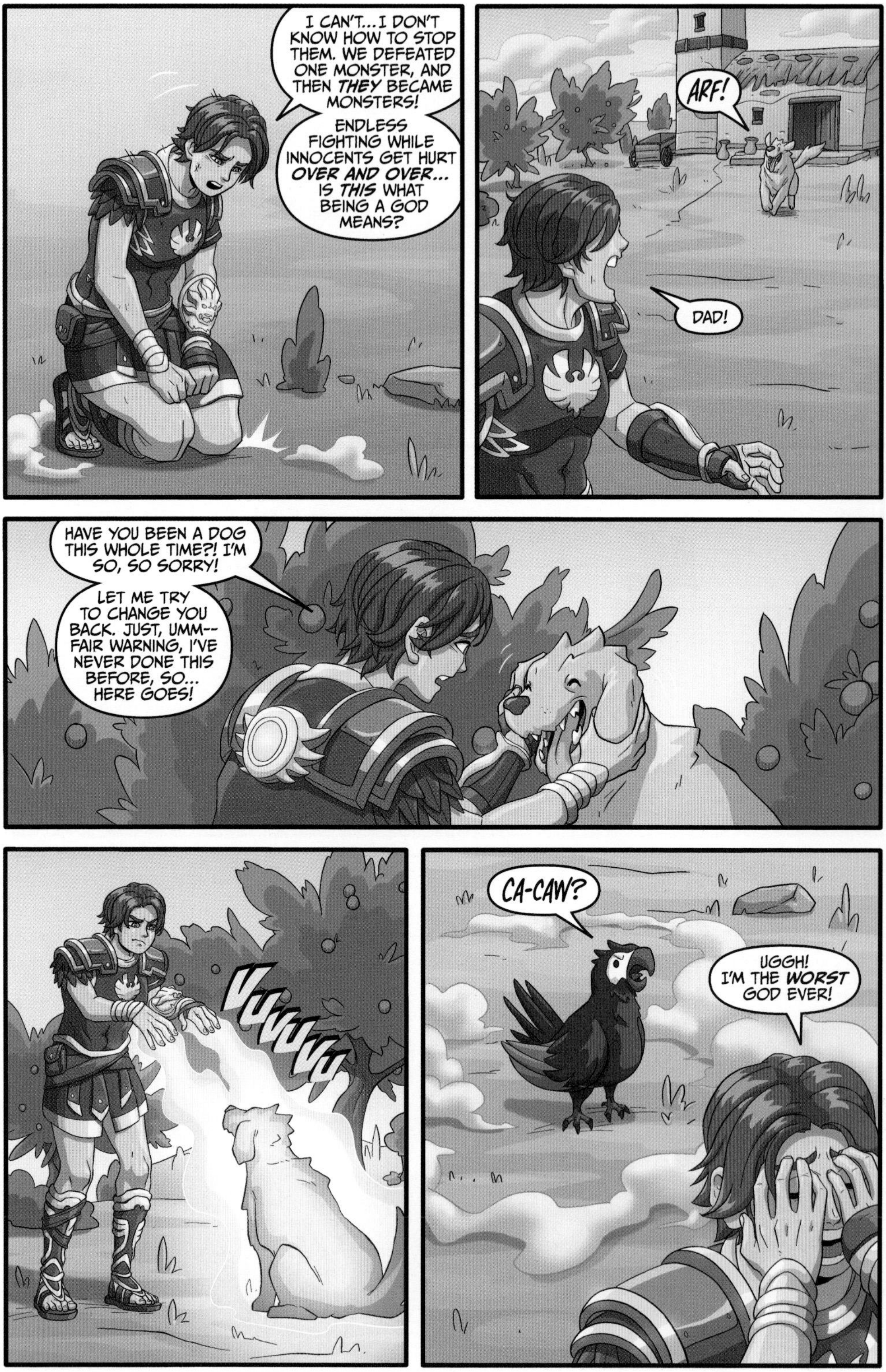
I CAN'T...I DON'T KNOW HOW TO STOP THEM. WE DEFEATED ONE MONSTER, AND THEN *THEY* BECAME MONSTERS!
ENDLESS FIGHTING WHILE INNOCENTS GET HURT *OVER AND OVER...* IS *THIS* WHAT BEING A GOD MEANS?
ARF!
DAD!
HAVE YOU BEEN A DOG THIS WHOLE TIME?! I'M SO, SO SORRY!
LET ME TRY TO CHANGE YOU BACK. JUST, UMM--FAIR WARNING, I'VE NEVER DONE THIS BEFORE, SO... HERE GOES!
VUVUVUVU
CA-CAW?
UGGH! I'M THE *WORST* GOD EVER!

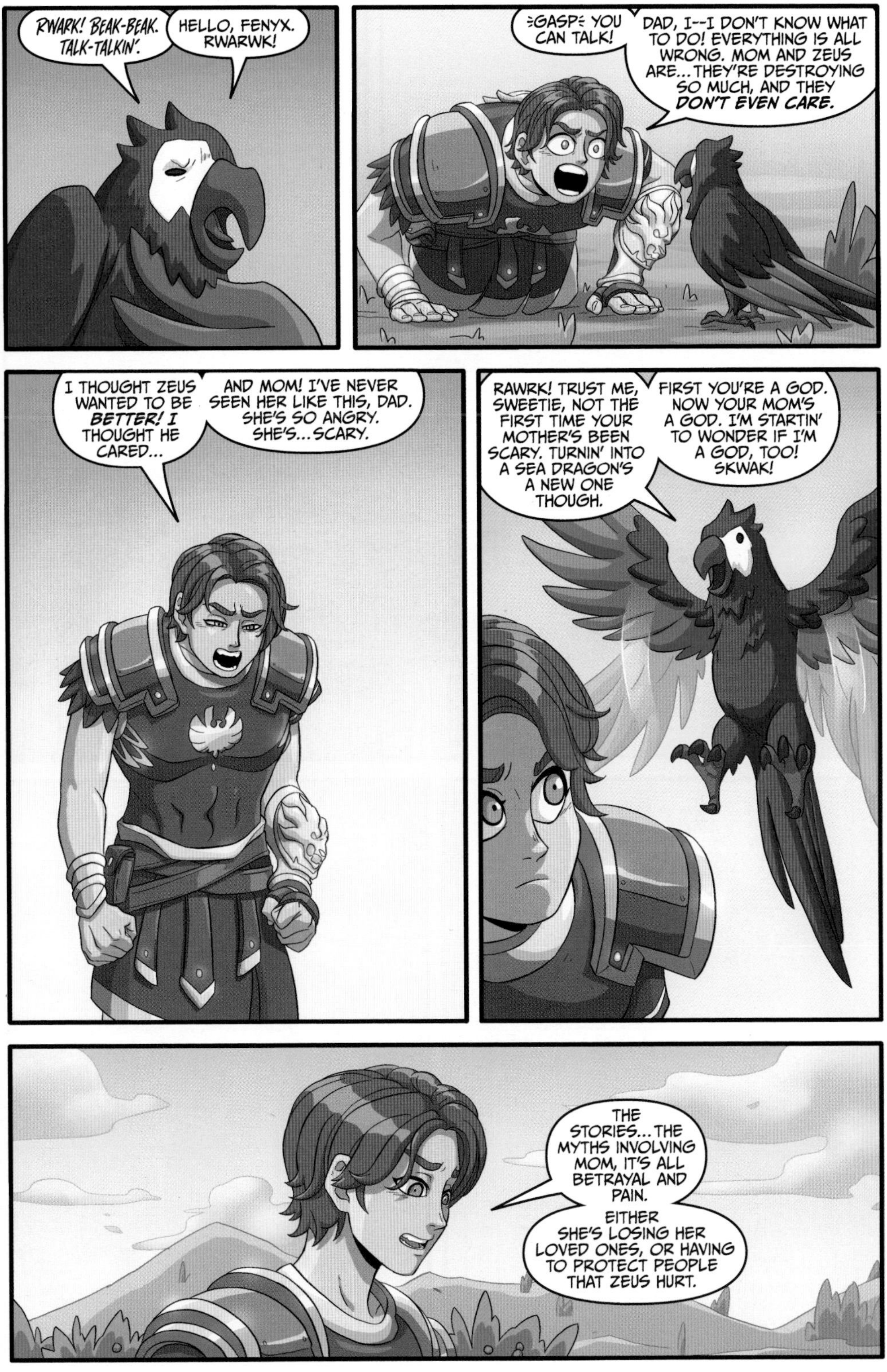
RWARK! BEAK-BEAK. TALK-TALKIN'.
HELLO, FENYX. RWARWK!
≑GASP≑ YOU CAN TALK!
DAD, I--I DON'T KNOW WHAT TO DO! EVERYTHING IS ALL WRONG. MOM AND ZEUS ARE... THEY'RE DESTROYING SO MUCH, AND THEY DON'T EVEN CARE.
I THOUGHT ZEUS WANTED TO BE BETTER! I THOUGHT HE CARED...
AND MOM! I'VE NEVER SEEN HER LIKE THIS, DAD. SHE'S SO ANGRY. SHE'S... SCARY.
RAWRK! TRUST ME, SWEETIE, NOT THE FIRST TIME YOUR MOTHER'S BEEN SCARY. TURNIN' INTO A SEA DRAGON'S A NEW ONE THOUGH.
FIRST YOU'RE A GOD. NOW YOUR MOM'S A GOD. I'M STARTIN' TO WONDER IF I'M A GOD, TOO! SKWAK!
THE STORIES... THE MYTHS INVOLVING MOM, IT'S ALL BETRAYAL AND PAIN.
EITHER SHE'S LOSING HER LOVED ONES, OR HAVING TO PROTECT PEOPLE THAT ZEUS HURT.

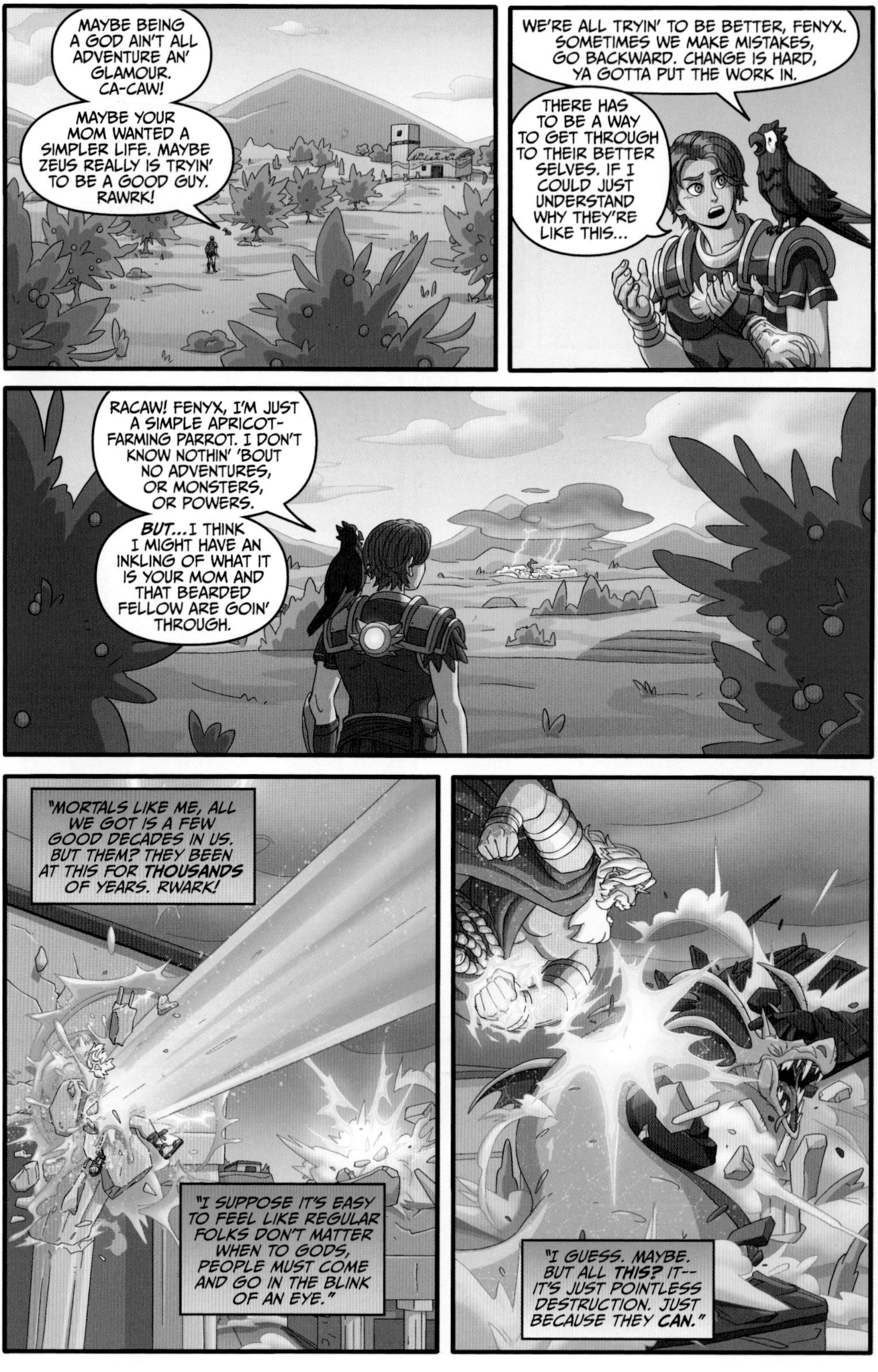
MAYBE BEING A GOD AIN'T ALL ADVENTURE AN' GLAMOUR. CA-CAW!
MAYBE YOUR MOM WANTED A SIMPLER LIFE. MAYBE ZEUS REALLY IS TRYIN' TO BE A GOOD GUY. RAWRK!
WE'RE ALL TRYIN' TO BE BETTER, FENYX. SOMETIMES WE MAKE MISTAKES, GO BACKWARD. CHANGE IS HARD, YA GOTTA PUT THE WORK IN.
THERE HAS TO BE A WAY TO GET THROUGH TO THEIR BETTER SELVES. IF I COULD JUST UNDERSTAND WHY THEY'RE LIKE THIS...
RACAW! FENYX, I'M JUST A SIMPLE APRICOT-FARMING PARROT. I DON'T KNOW NOTHIN' 'BOUT NO ADVENTURES, OR MONSTERS, OR POWERS.
BUT... I THINK I MIGHT HAVE AN INKLING OF WHAT IT IS YOUR MOM AND THAT BEARDED FELLOW ARE GOIN' THROUGH.
"MORTALS LIKE ME, ALL WE GOT IS A FEW GOOD DECADES IN US. BUT THEM? THEY BEEN AT THIS FOR **THOUSANDS** OF YEARS. RWARK!
"I SUPPOSE IT'S EASY TO FEEL LIKE REGULAR FOLKS DON'T MATTER WHEN TO GODS, PEOPLE MUST COME AND GO IN THE BLINK OF AN EYE."
"I GUESS. MAYBE. BUT ALL **THIS?** IT-- IT'S JUST POINTLESS DESTRUCTION. JUST BECAUSE THEY **CAN.**"

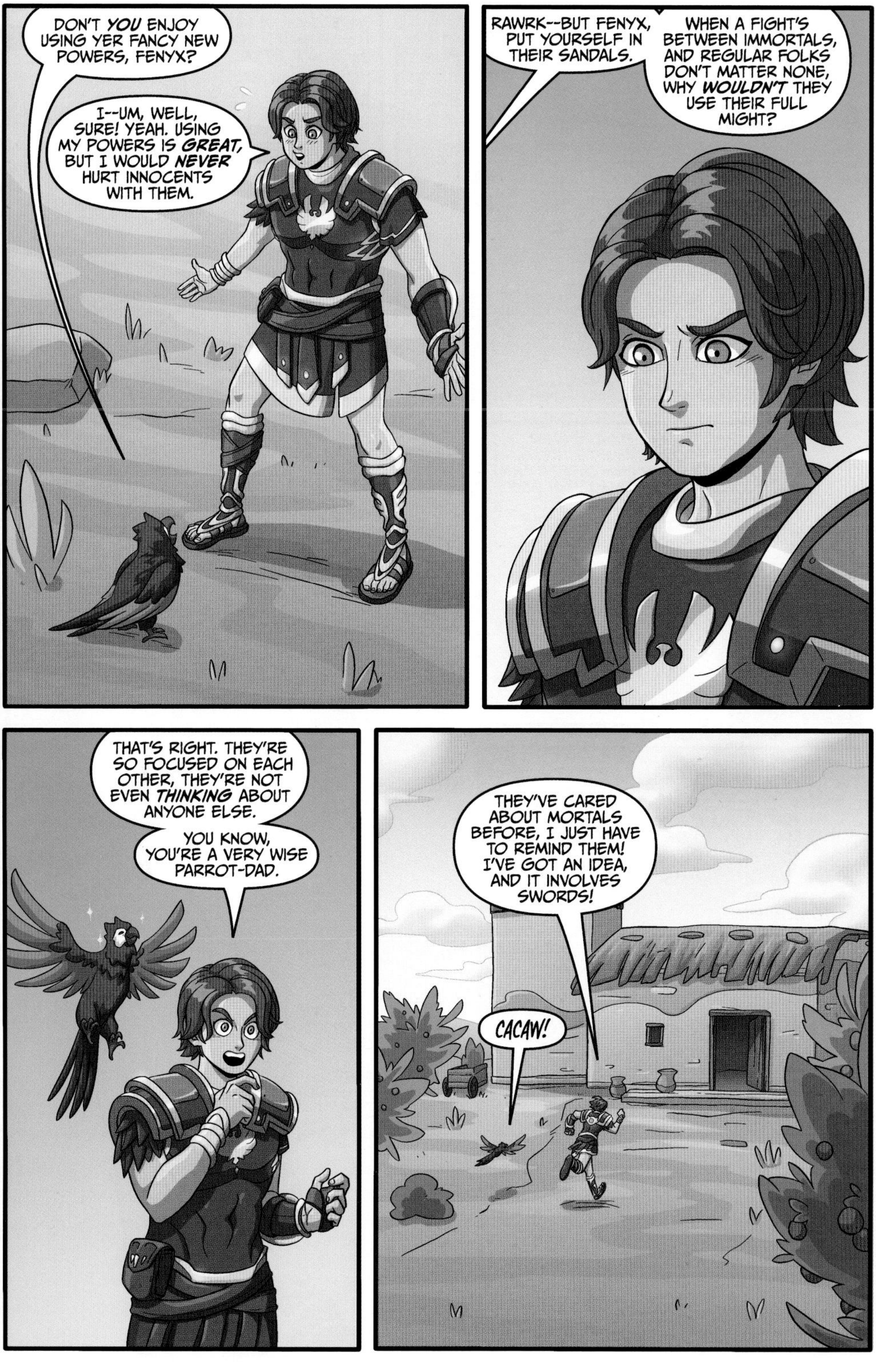
DON'T *YOU* ENJOY USING YER FANCY NEW POWERS, FENYX?
I--UM, WELL, SURE! YEAH. USING MY POWERS IS *GREAT*, BUT I WOULD *NEVER* HURT INNOCENTS WITH THEM.
RAWRK--BUT FENYX, PUT YOURSELF IN THEIR SANDALS.
WHEN A FIGHT'S BETWEEN IMMORTALS, AND REGULAR FOLKS DON'T MATTER NONE, WHY *WOULDN'T* THEY USE THEIR FULL MIGHT?
THAT'S RIGHT. THEY'RE SO FOCUSED ON EACH OTHER, THEY'RE NOT EVEN *THINKING* ABOUT ANYONE ELSE.
YOU KNOW, YOU'RE A VERY WISE PARROT-DAD.
THEY'VE CARED ABOUT MORTALS BEFORE, I JUST HAVE TO REMIND THEM! I'VE GOT AN IDEA, AND IT INVOLVES SWORDS!
CACAW!

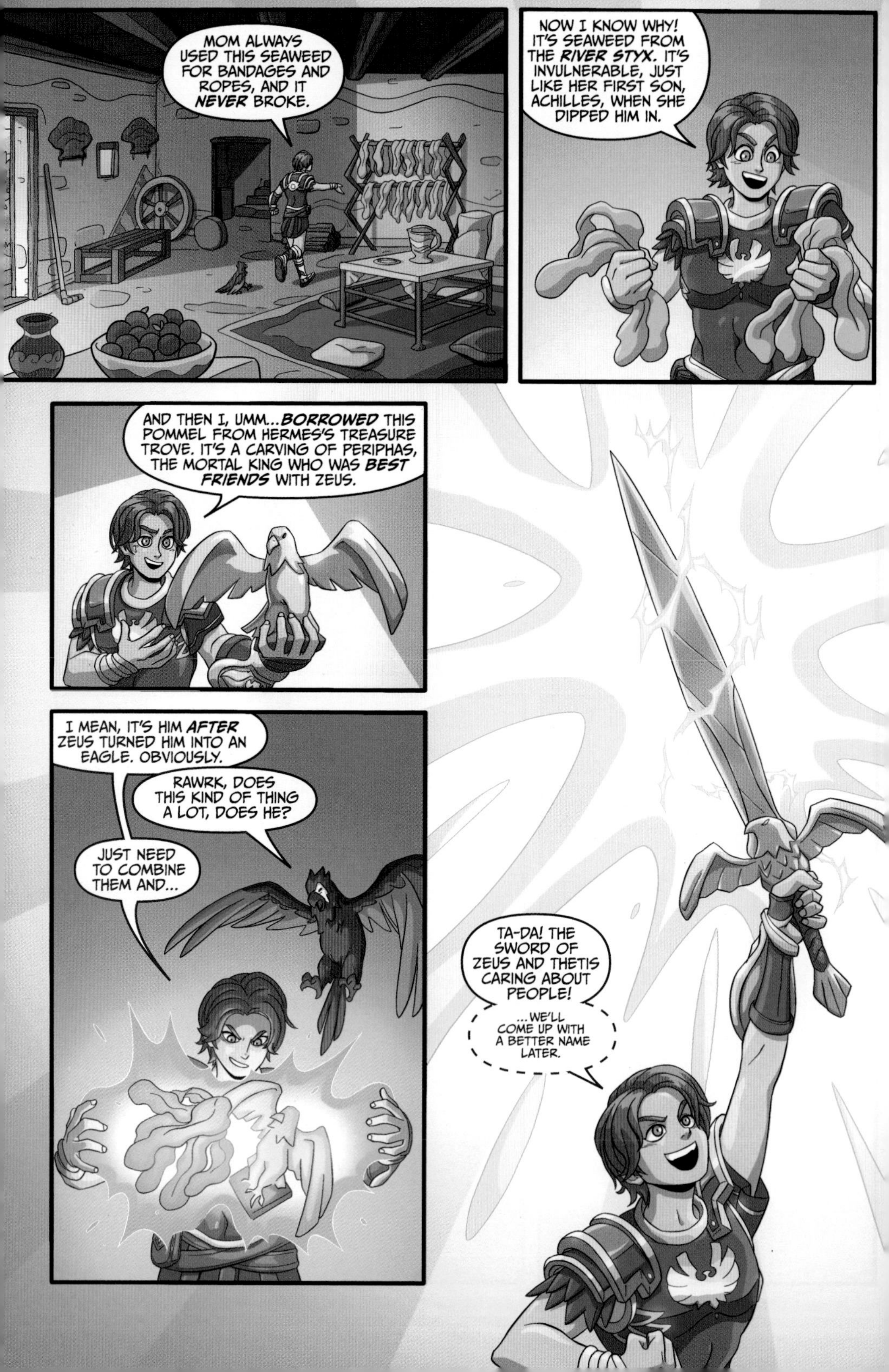
MOM ALWAYS USED THIS SEAWEED FOR BANDAGES AND ROPES, AND IT NEVER BROKE.
NOW I KNOW WHY! IT'S SEAWEED FROM THE RIVER STYX. IT'S INVULNERABLE, JUST LIKE HER FIRST SON, ACHILLES, WHEN SHE DIPPED HIM IN.
AND THEN I, UMM...BORROWED THIS POMMEL FROM HERMES'S TREASURE TROVE. IT'S A CARVING OF PERIPHAS, THE MORTAL KING WHO WAS BEST FRIENDS WITH ZEUS.
I MEAN, IT'S HIM AFTER ZEUS TURNED HIM INTO AN EAGLE. OBVIOUSLY.
RAWRK, DOES THIS KIND OF THING A LOT, DOES HE?
JUST NEED TO COMBINE THEM AND...
TA-DA! THE SWORD OF ZEUS AND THETIS CARING ABOUT PEOPLE!
...WE'LL COME UP WITH A BETTER NAME LATER.

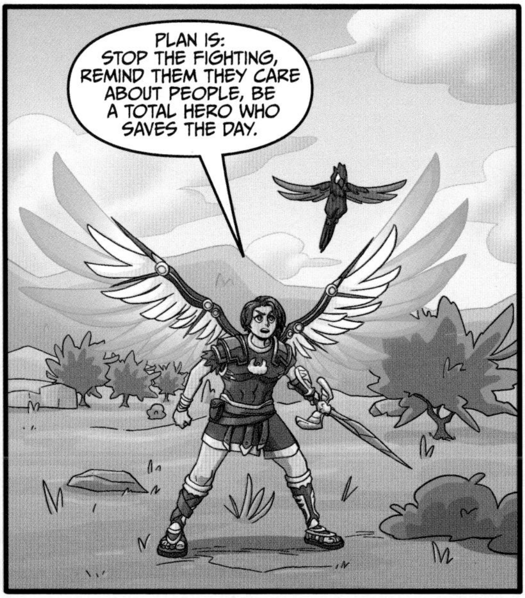
PLAN IS: STOP THE FIGHTING, REMIND THEM THEY CARE ABOUT PEOPLE, BE A TOTAL HERO WHO SAVES THE DAY.

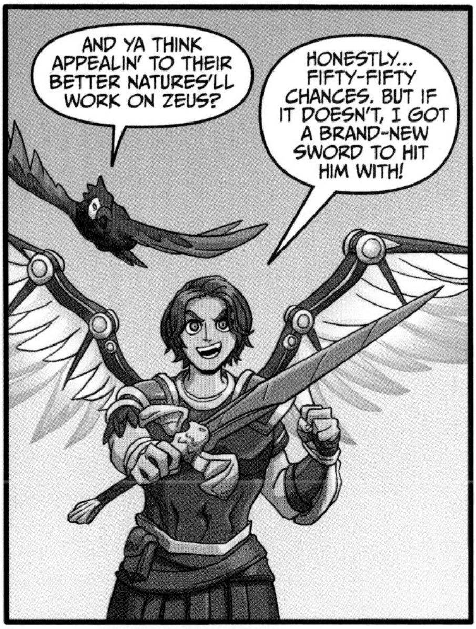
AND YA THINK APPEALIN' TO THEIR BETTER NATURES'LL WORK ON ZEUS?
HONESTLY... FIFTY-FIFTY CHANCES. BUT IF IT DOESN'T, I GOT A BRAND-NEW SWORD TO HIT HIM WITH!

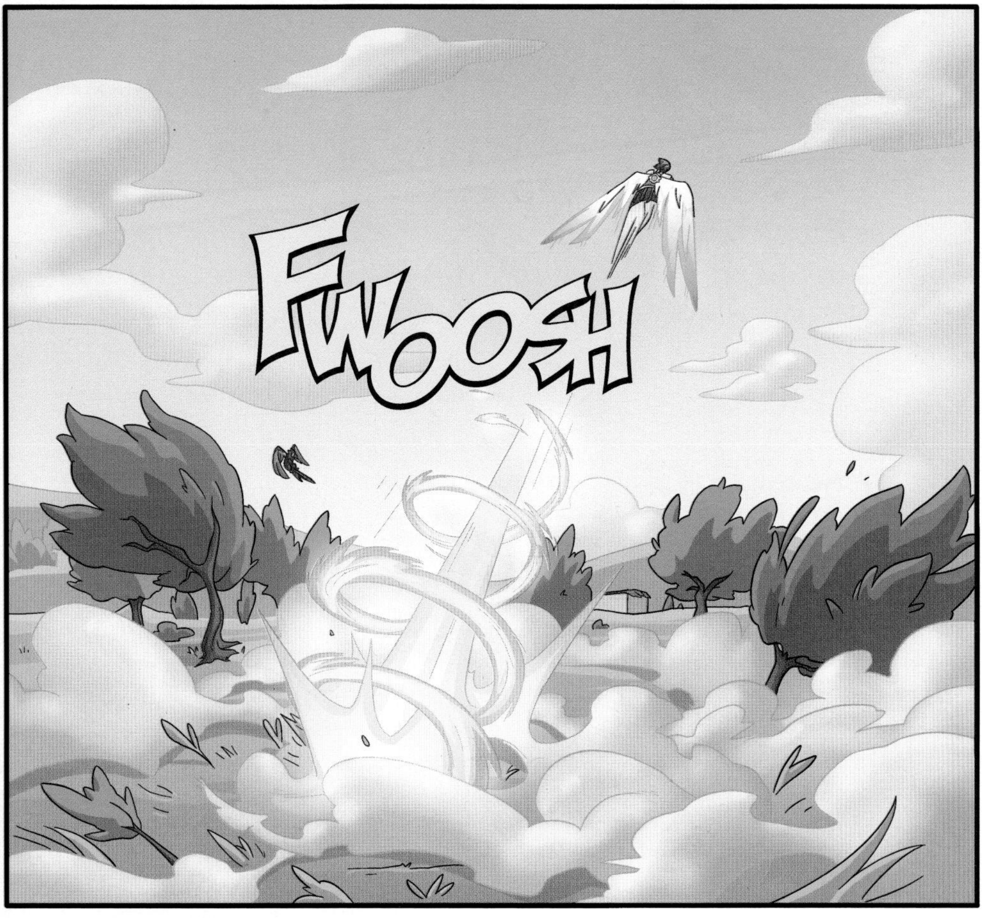
FWOOSH

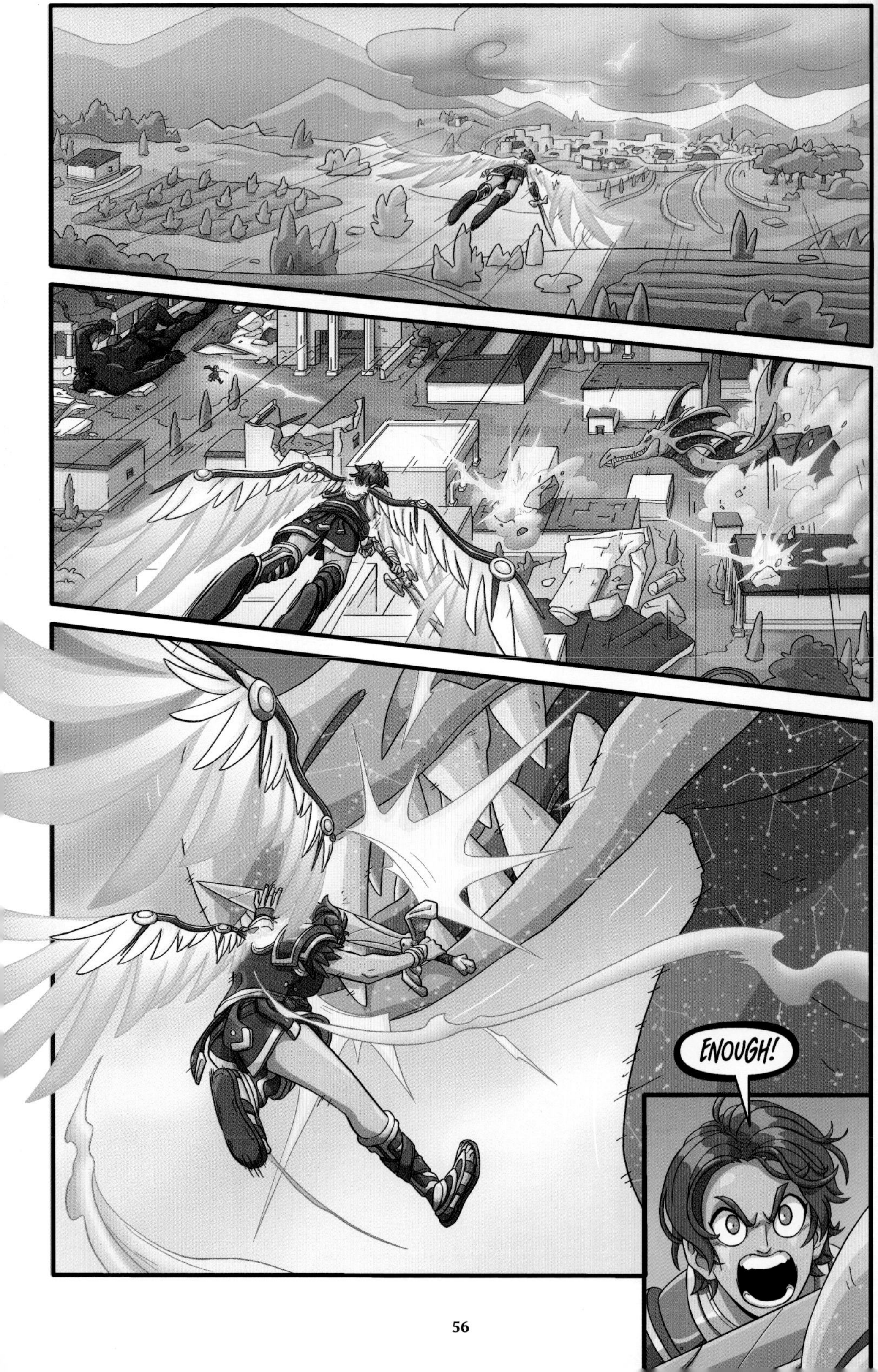
ENOUGH!

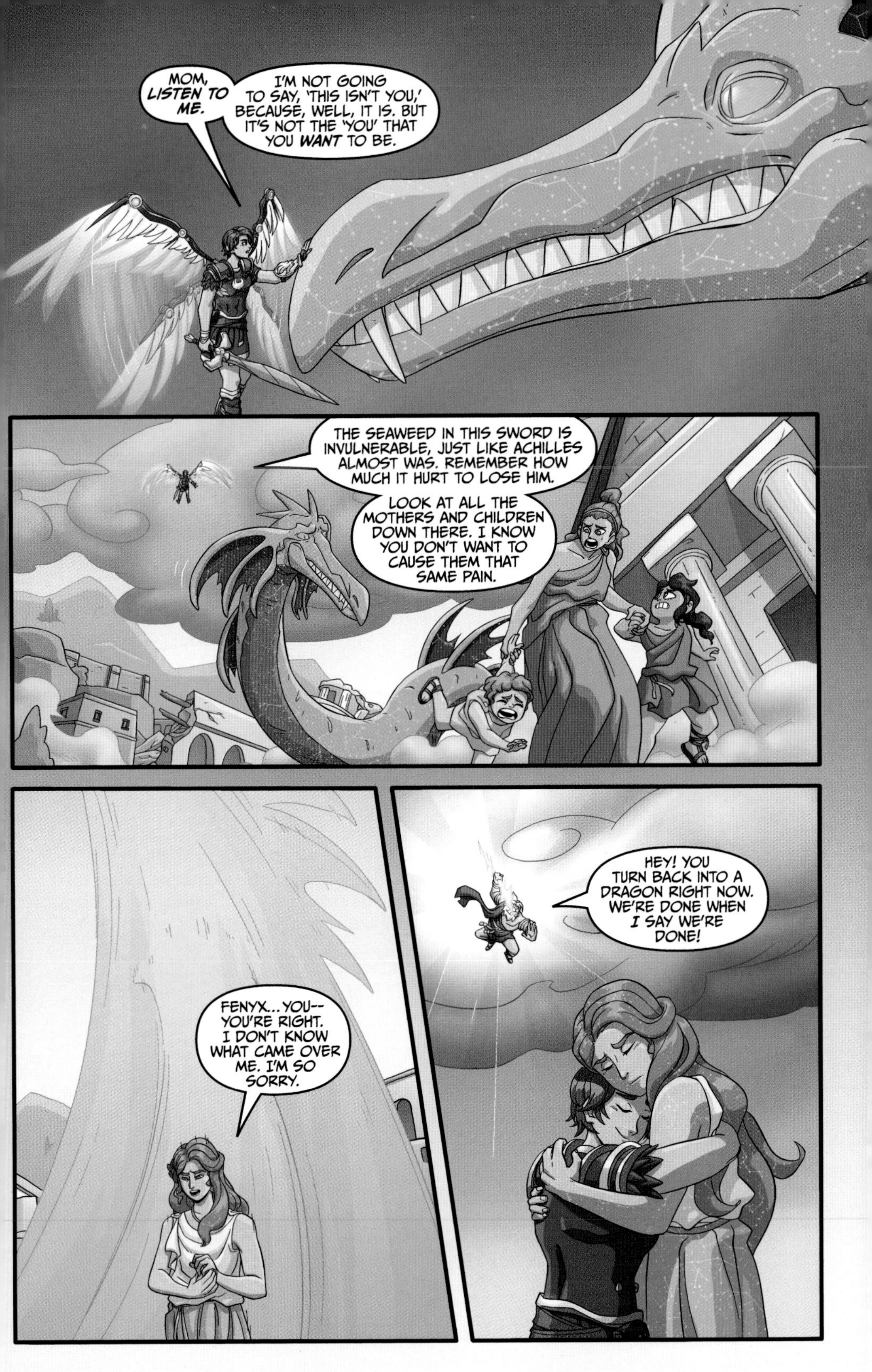
MOM, LISTEN TO ME.
I'M NOT GOING TO SAY, 'THIS ISN'T YOU,' BECAUSE, WELL, IT IS. BUT IT'S NOT THE 'YOU' THAT YOU WANT TO BE.
THE SEAWEED IN THIS SWORD IS INVULNERABLE, JUST LIKE ACHILLES ALMOST WAS. REMEMBER HOW MUCH IT HURT TO LOSE HIM.
LOOK AT ALL THE MOTHERS AND CHILDREN DOWN THERE. I KNOW YOU DON'T WANT TO CAUSE THEM THAT SAME PAIN.
FENYX... YOU-- YOU'RE RIGHT. I DON'T KNOW WHAT CAME OVER ME. I'M SO SORRY.
HEY! YOU TURN BACK INTO A DRAGON RIGHT NOW. WE'RE DONE WHEN I SAY WE'RE DONE!

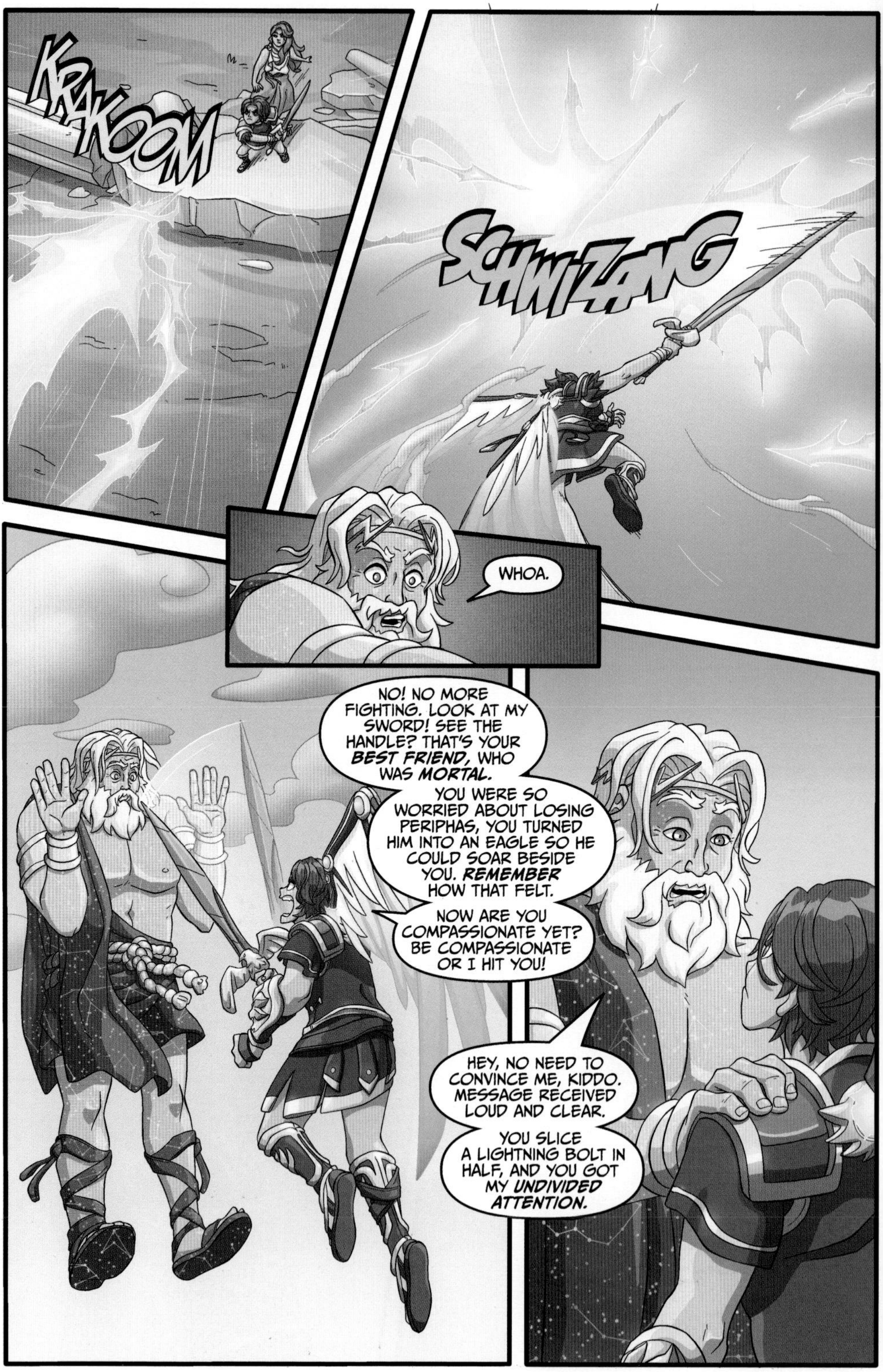
KRAKOOM
SCHWIZANG
WHOA.
NO! NO MORE FIGHTING. LOOK AT MY SWORD! SEE THE HANDLE? THAT'S YOUR **BEST FRIEND,** WHO WAS **MORTAL.**
YOU WERE SO WORRIED ABOUT LOSING PERIPHAS, YOU TURNED HIM INTO AN EAGLE SO HE COULD SOAR BESIDE YOU. **REMEMBER** HOW THAT FELT.
NOW ARE YOU COMPASSIONATE YET? BE COMPASSIONATE OR I HIT YOU!
HEY, NO NEED TO CONVINCE ME, KIDDO. MESSAGE RECEIVED LOUD AND CLEAR.
YOU SLICE A LIGHTNING BOLT IN HALF, AND YOU GOT MY ***UNDIVIDED ATTENTION.***

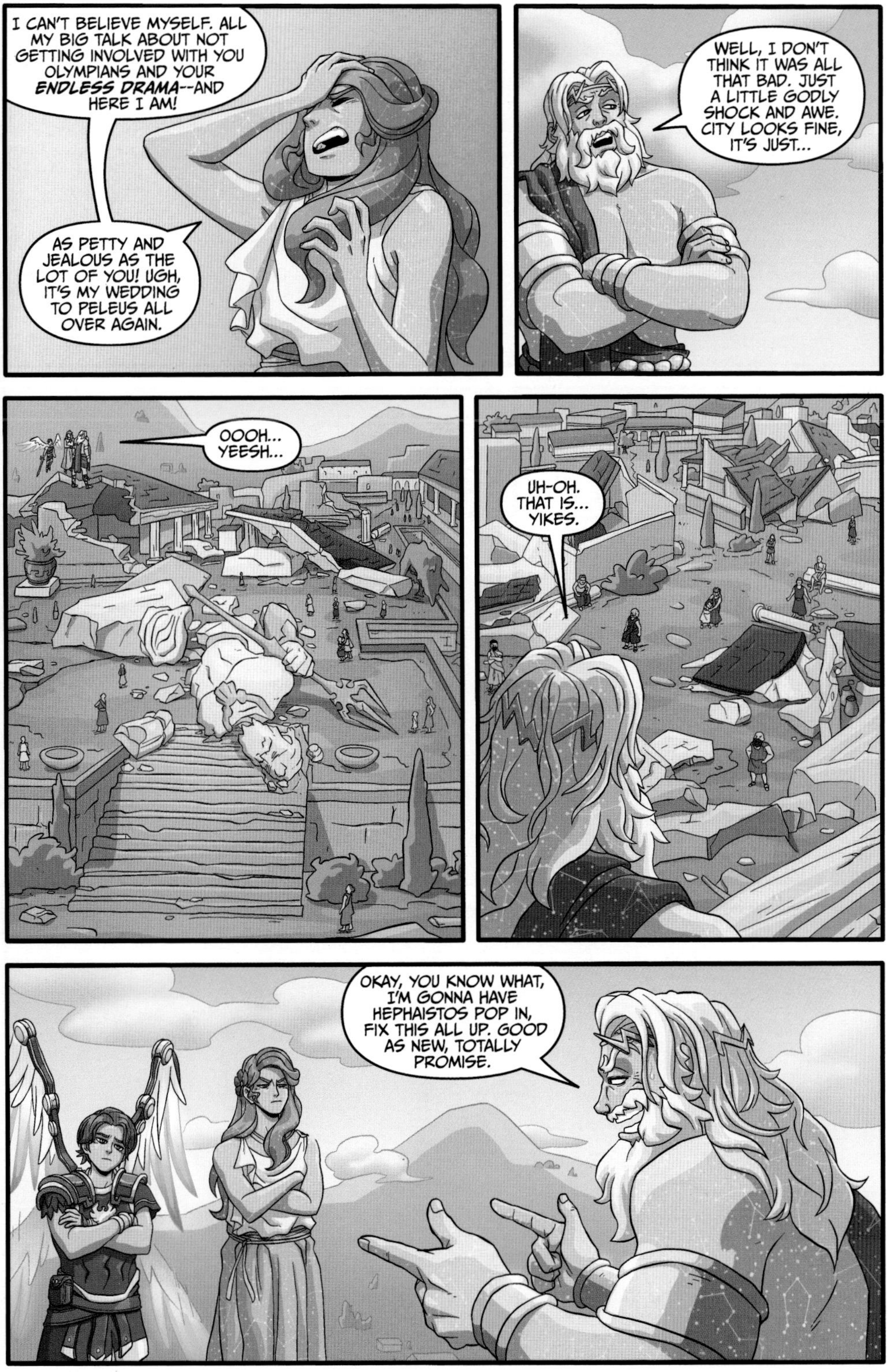
I CAN'T BELIEVE MYSELF. ALL MY BIG TALK ABOUT NOT GETTING INVOLVED WITH YOU OLYMPIANS AND YOUR ENDLESS DRAMA--AND HERE I AM!
AS PETTY AND JEALOUS AS THE LOT OF YOU! UGH, IT'S MY WEDDING TO PELEUS ALL OVER AGAIN.
WELL, I DON'T THINK IT WAS ALL THAT BAD. JUST A LITTLE GODLY SHOCK AND AWE. CITY LOOKS FINE, IT'S JUST...
OOOH... YEESH...
UH-OH. THAT IS... YIKES.
OKAY, YOU KNOW WHAT, I'M GONNA HAVE HEPHAISTOS POP IN, FIX THIS ALL UP. GOOD AS NEW, TOTALLY PROMISE.

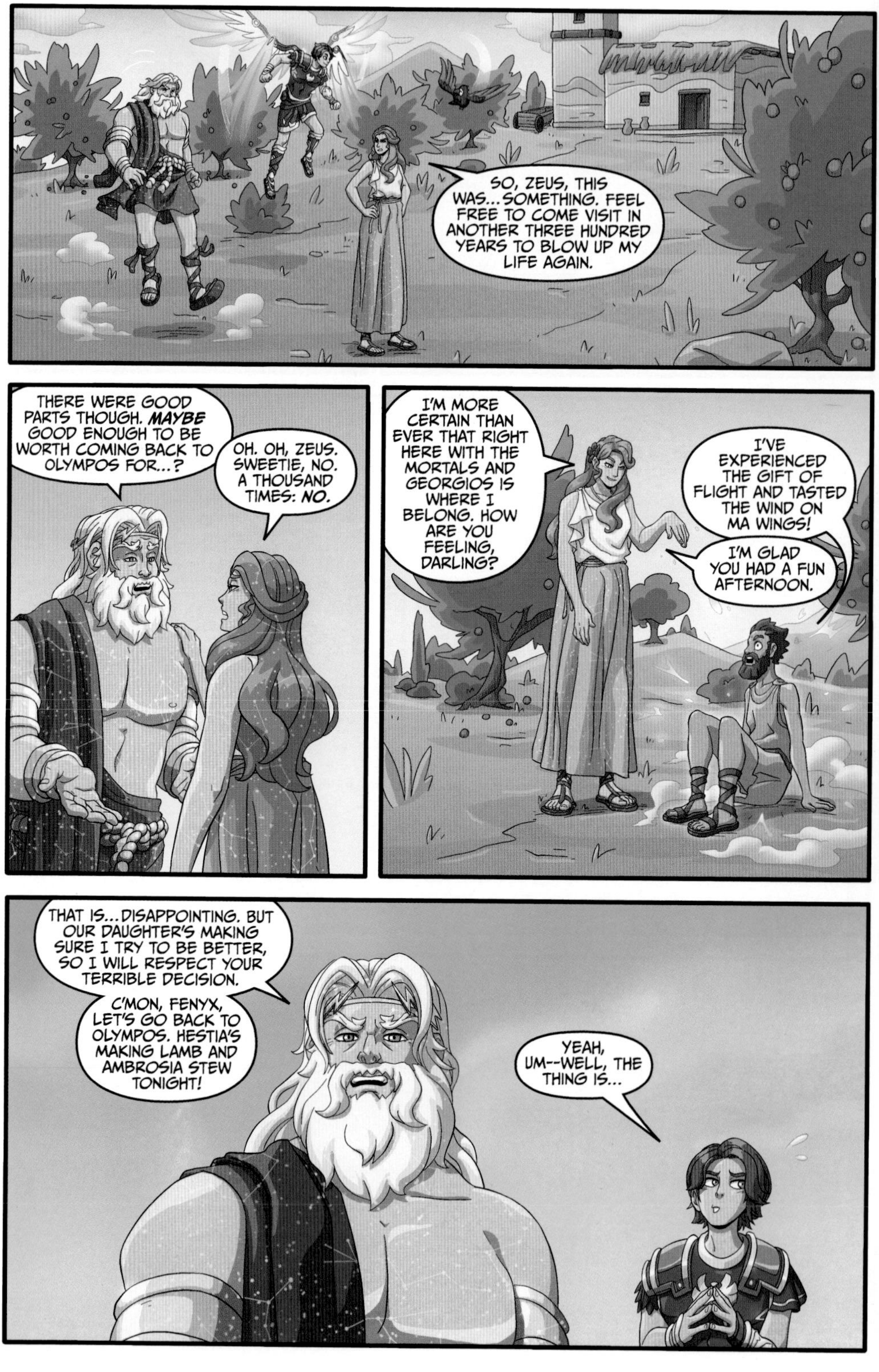
SO, ZEUS, THIS WAS... SOMETHING. FEEL FREE TO COME VISIT IN ANOTHER THREE HUNDRED YEARS TO BLOW UP MY LIFE AGAIN.
THERE WERE GOOD PARTS THOUGH. MAYBE GOOD ENOUGH TO BE WORTH COMING BACK TO OLYMPOS FOR...?
OH. OH, ZEUS. SWEETIE, NO. A THOUSAND TIMES: NO.
I'M MORE CERTAIN THAN EVER THAT RIGHT HERE WITH THE MORTALS AND GEORGIOS IS WHERE I BELONG. HOW ARE YOU FEELING, DARLING?
I'VE EXPERIENCED THE GIFT OF FLIGHT AND TASTED THE WIND ON MA WINGS!
I'M GLAD YOU HAD A FUN AFTERNOON.
THAT IS... DISAPPOINTING. BUT OUR DAUGHTER'S MAKING SURE I TRY TO BE BETTER, SO I WILL RESPECT YOUR TERRIBLE DECISION.
C'MON, FENYX, LET'S GO BACK TO OLYMPOS. HESTIA'S MAKING LAMB AND AMBROSIA STEW TONIGHT!
YEAH, UM--WELL, THE THING IS...

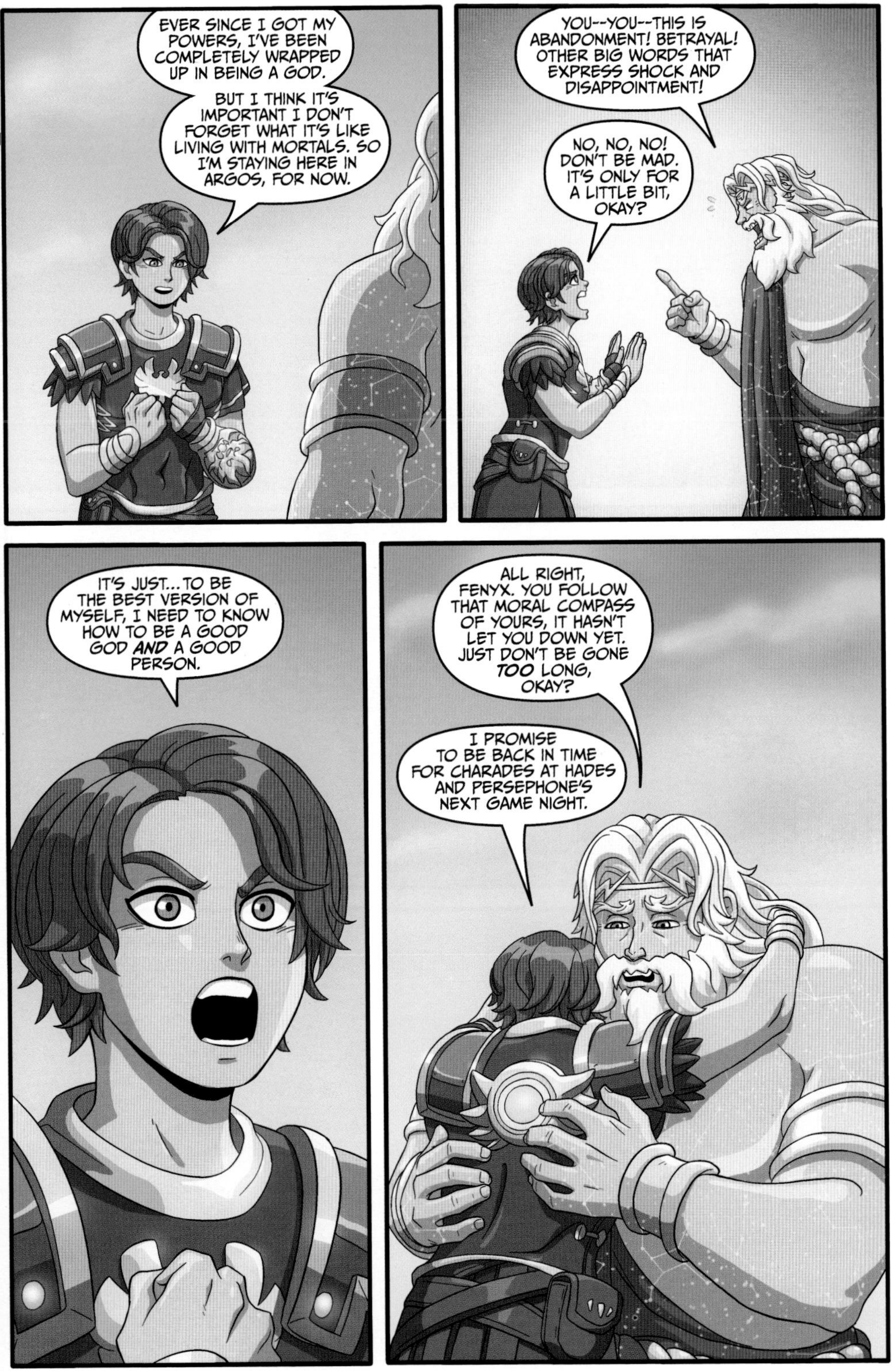
EVER SINCE I GOT MY POWERS, I'VE BEEN COMPLETELY WRAPPED UP IN BEING A GOD.
BUT I THINK IT'S IMPORTANT I DON'T FORGET WHAT IT'S LIKE LIVING WITH MORTALS. SO I'M STAYING HERE IN ARGOS, FOR NOW.
YOU--YOU--THIS IS ABANDONMENT! BETRAYAL! OTHER BIG WORDS THAT EXPRESS SHOCK AND DISAPPOINTMENT!
NO, NO, NO! DON'T BE MAD. IT'S ONLY FOR A LITTLE BIT, OKAY?
IT'S JUST...TO BE THE BEST VERSION OF MYSELF, I NEED TO KNOW HOW TO BE A GOOD GOD **AND** A GOOD PERSON.
ALL RIGHT, FENYX. YOU FOLLOW THAT MORAL COMPASS OF YOURS, IT HASN'T LET YOU DOWN YET. JUST DON'T BE GONE **TOO** LONG, OKAY?
I PROMISE TO BE BACK IN TIME FOR CHARADES AT HADES AND PERSEPHONE'S NEXT GAME NIGHT.

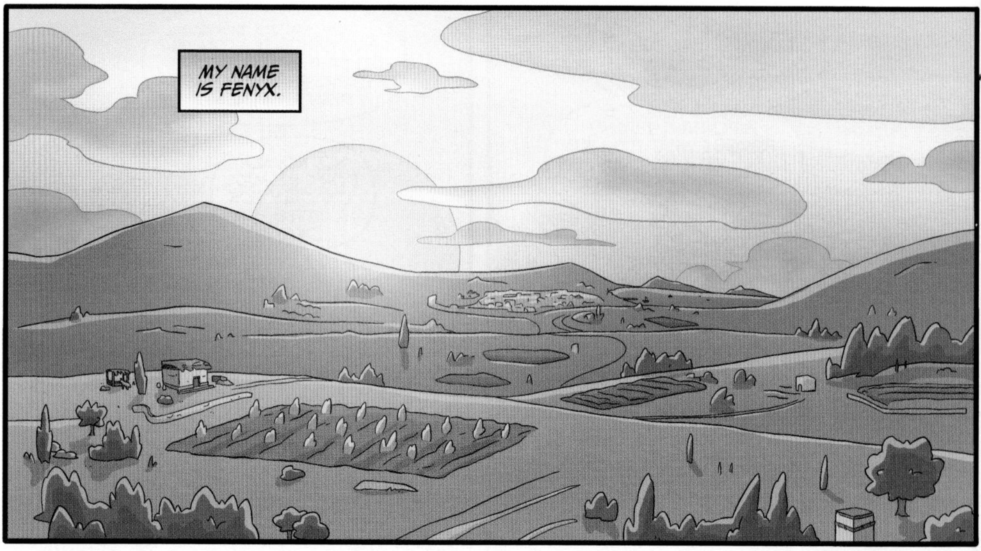
MY NAME
IS FENYX.

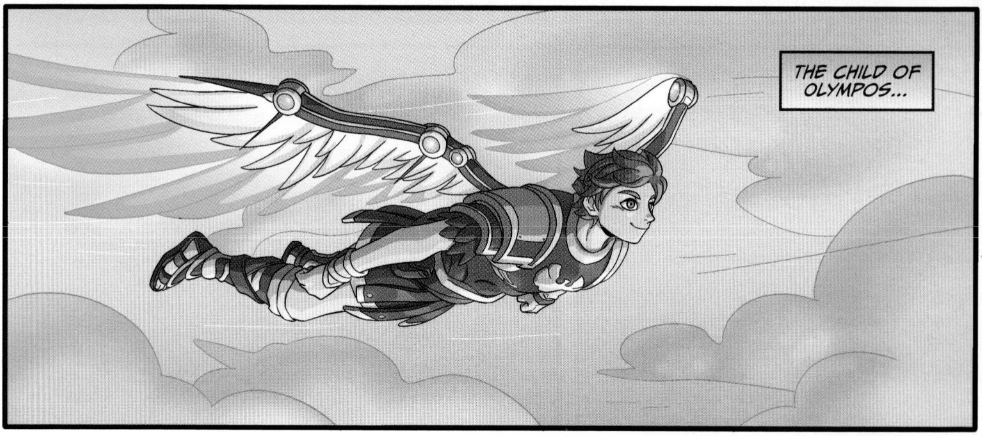
THE CHILD OF
OLYMPOS...

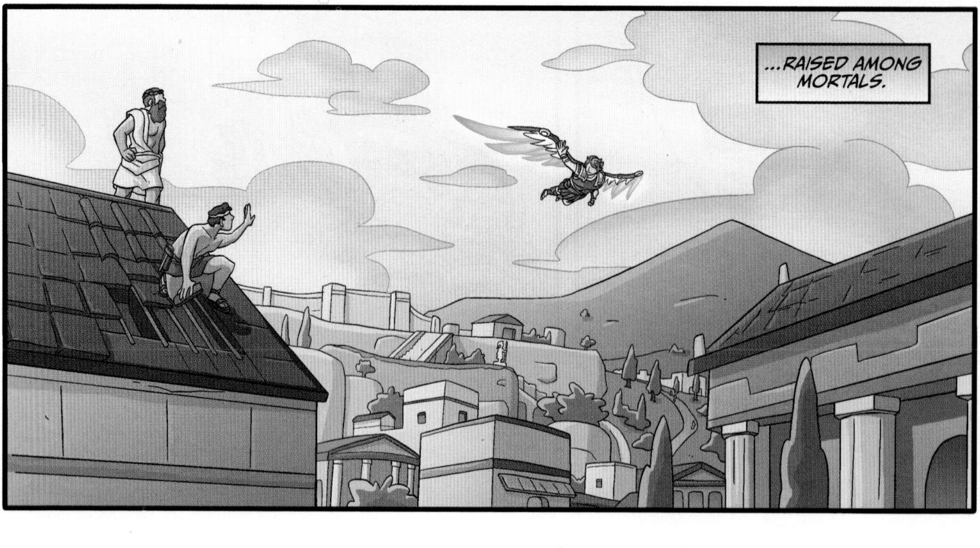
...RAISED AMONG
MORTALS.

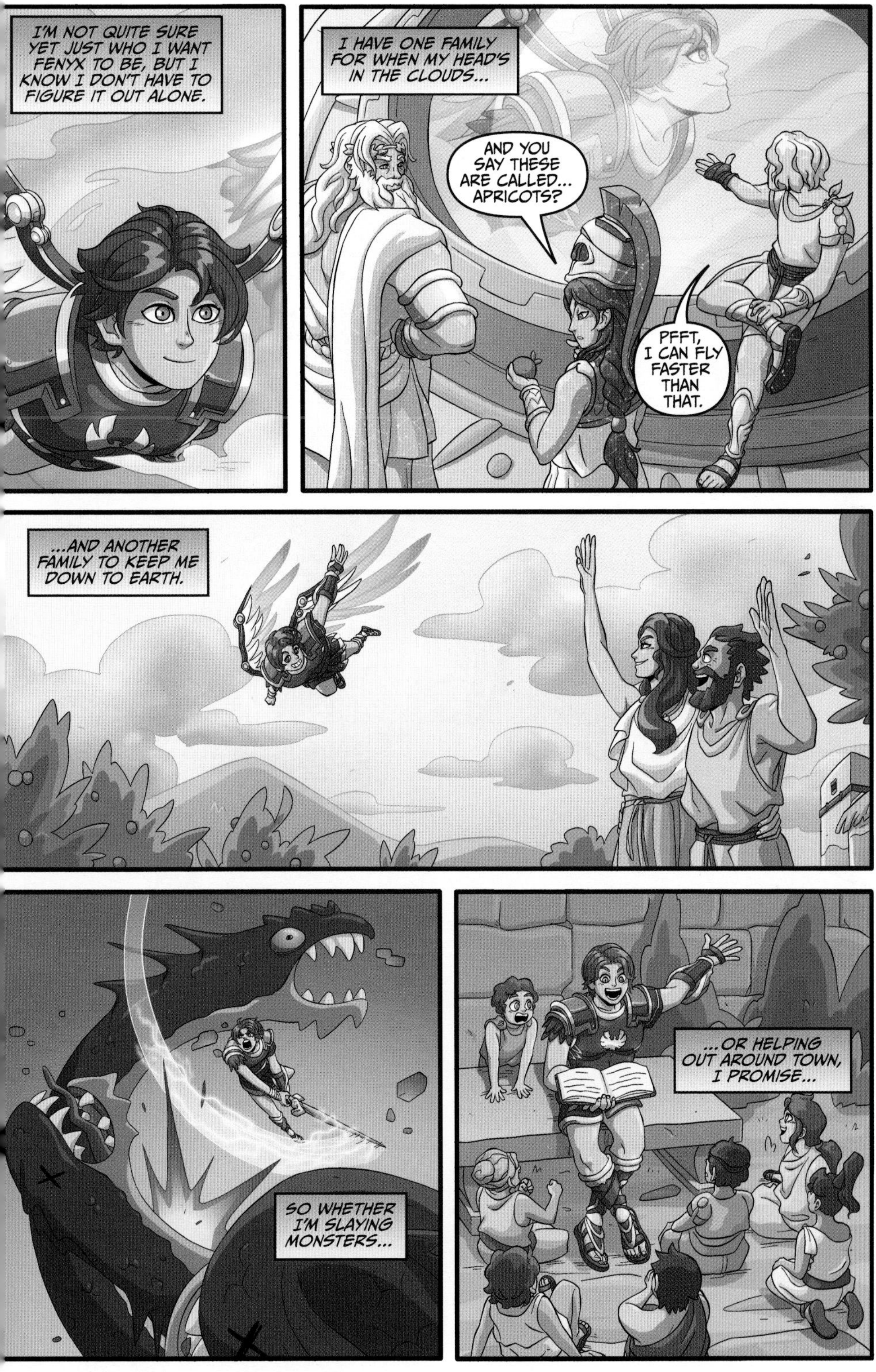
I'M NOT QUITE SURE YET JUST WHO I WANT FENYX TO BE, BUT I KNOW I DON'T HAVE TO FIGURE IT OUT ALONE.
I HAVE ONE FAMILY FOR WHEN MY HEAD'S IN THE CLOUDS...
AND YOU SAY THESE ARE CALLED... APRICOTS?
PFFT, I CAN FLY FASTER THAN THAT.
...AND ANOTHER FAMILY TO KEEP ME DOWN TO EARTH.
SO WHETHER I'M SLAYING MONSTERS...
...OR HELPING OUT AROUND TOWN, I PROMISE...

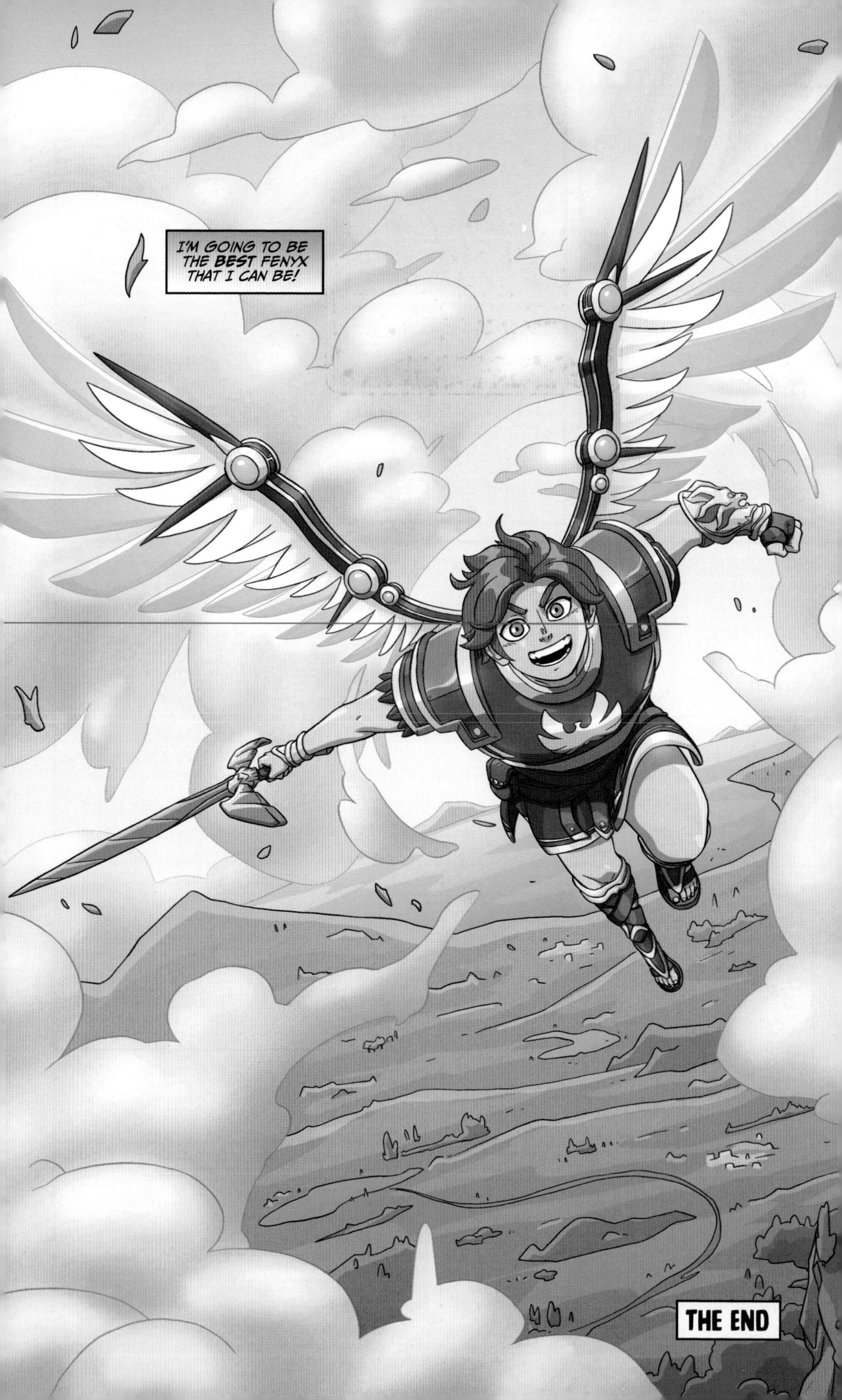
I'M GOING TO BE THE **BEST** FENYX THAT I CAN BE!
THE END